Lost Boys
Never
Say Die

Lost Boys Never Say Die

ALAN BROWN
and
GRANT FORSBERG

Delacorte Press

Published by Delacorte Press
Bantam Doubleday Dell Publishing Group, Inc.
666 Fifth Avenue
New York, New York 10103

Library of Congress Cataloging in Publication Data

Brown, Alan M.
Lost boys never say die / by Alan M. Brown
and Grant E. Forsberg.
p. cm.
Summary: Scheduled to go to summer camp to work on his stuttering problem while his parents go off to the Arctic, Lewis surreptitiously steals back into his house where he lives a secret life for eight weeks, meeting a new friend who is camping in a nearby woods and who involves Lewis in acting and a new approach to his speech problem and to life.

ISBN 0-385-29781-5
[1. Stuttering—Fiction.] I. Forsberg, Grant E.
II. Title. PZ7.B81264Lo 1989
[Fic]—dc19
88-36419 CIP AC

Designed by Andrew Roberts

Manufactured in the United States of America

September 1989

10 9 8 7 6 5 4 3 2 1

BG

For Jessica

A.B.

For Beverly S.

G.F.

Contents

1

Camp Chicopee

LEWIS DEE WALKED HOME ALONE. As usual. All around him his classmates could hardly contain their excitement. And for once they didn't have to. Not today. School was finally over. Finished. A whole summer of freedom stretched before them. They were like prisoners seeing the light of day for the first time in years, Lewis mused as he watched them running down the street. Lewis imagined himself with the other boys from his sixth-grade class, dashing behind the teachers' cars in the school parking lot, hiding and jumping out to scare the girls.

And then, out of the corner of his eye, he caught sight of Stanley Flynn, North Renfield's resident bully. Flynn was, as usual, flanked by his gang—the Kaminsky twins, Wanker and Cheese, followed by Cueball Lebowitz, and, bringing up the rear, Cycle Griffiths, the only girl—if you could call her that —in Flynn's gang. Cycle had a crew cut and wore at least eight earrings in each ear, plus a ring through her nose. She even had a chain connecting the nose ring to one of the earrings. As if that weren't enough, she always wore a leather dog collar around her neck with real metal studs in it. Cycle Griffiths. Pretty heavy-duty stuff for North Renfield.

"Hey, little L-L-L-Lewis," Flynn mimicked as he stuck his big ugly head right in Lewis's face. "Where do you think you're going?"

Words stuck in Lewis's throat. He couldn't speak. He couldn't move. It was as if everything in his body had turned to stone.

"Hey, L-L-L-Lewis," Flynn started in again, poking him in the chest, shoving him backward. "I asked you a question, retard."

"Ha-ha, retard! Little retarded punk," Cycle said with a laugh.

Flynn continued pushing Lewis until he backed him up into Cueball, who was down on his hands and knees on the sidewalk behind him. Lewis fell over backward and Flynn cracked up. The rest of the gang burst out laughing too. They always had to do exactly what Flynn did.

"Hey, c-c-c-creep, here's one to remember me by," Flynn said. He gave Lewis a kick in the ribs and then strutted off with his gang.

"See ya in September, retard," Wanker shouted. Then he and his brother, Cheese, ran off, chasing some girls and knocking their schoolbooks to the ground.

Lewis was left lying there, crying, his knees pulled up to his chest for protection. Other kids were looking at him, so he closed his eyes and rolled off the sidewalk onto the grass. Humiliated and afraid that a teacher might see him, he lay that way for a long time, until he was sure that all of the other kids were gone, until everything was quiet.

Lewis was a stutterer, so he'd been teased and mimicked ever since he was little. Rubber bands, paper clips, spitballs, stones, paper airplanes—you name it—everything airborne had been aimed at his head. He'd had gum stuck in his hair, he'd been pushed, poked, kicked, and tripped. He'd even had his head shoved into a toilet bowl. He couldn't count the times his lunch money had been taken away from him.

The worst had definitely been in Detroit. No contest. He was in the fourth grade when some crazy kid pushed him up against the lockers in the school hallway and set fire to his down jacket. If it hadn't been for the quick thinking of a passing teacher, Lewis would have been badly burned. Boy, he didn't miss living in Detroit.

Lewis's father was a consulting engineer (a title Lewis had yet to pronounce without stuttering), and the Dees had had to move frequently because of his work. For Lewis this meant always being the "new kid" in a new school, with new bullies and new ways of being teased and tormented. Each time they moved, he hoped it would be different, but it never was. It was as if the bullies at his old school called the bullies at his new school to let them know that he was on his way.

Walking home now, Lewis didn't think about what had just happened. He was good at that—a necessary survival skill. Instead, he thought of the summer ahead.

Lewis loved summer vacations. He loved everything about them: the warm weather, the freedom, being away from the jerks at school. But most of all he loved the traveling. Ever since he was a little boy, Lewis and his mother had joined his father on summer trips while he worked on bridges and buildings and roadways all over the world.

This summer was going to be the most exciting ever because they were headed for the Arctic, where his father would be working on some special research station for scientists from all different countries. Lewis and his mother had been preparing for this trip the way they always prepared for their trips—by reading books. But even with all of the books, he couldn't imagine what it would be like at "the kingdom at the end of the world." He'd read that the Arctic was the coldest, highest, and driest place on earth, and in all of the pictures it looked like millions of miles of ice, everything completely white and quiet. Lewis imagined that there would be penguins and ferocious polar bears everywhere, and that everybody would walk around in heavy down suits with goggles and fur hoods. Next week, in fact, he and his parents were driving into New York City to go shopping for the special warm clothes they'd need.

Lewis figured that at eleven he'd seen more of the world than most people ever see of their own countries. Certainly more than Stanley Flynn would ever see. He couldn't even seem to see the seventh grade. Flynn had been held back twice, and at the rate he was going, he was likely to be the first boy in the elementary school to have a driver's license. Lewis thought about Flynn being stuck in the sixth grade for the rest of his life, still sitting at the very front of the room where the teacher could keep an eye on him, an old man with a white beard, his long grown-up legs crammed painfully under the small desk.

Lewis's fantasies ended as he neared the bend in the railroad tracks that ran through North Renfield. Looking in both directions, he cut through some prickly bushes and onto a side street that looped around the tracks, walking about a half mile out of his way. Flynn and his gang often hung out by that particular bend after school, smoking cigarettes. And now that the weather was warm enough for swimming, they would jump trains as they slowed down for the bend, hitching a free ride north to the quarry where the high-school kids went to swim and drink beer. Lewis had no desire to bump into Flynn again.

* * *

THE DEE FAMILY had lived in North Renfield, a small college town on the Hudson River in New York state, only since Christmas. Lewis's mother had found a part-time job teaching ceramics in the art department of the college. His father commuted to his company's headquarters in New York City, or else traveled to special jobs.

When they'd first moved into the old shingled house on the edge of the woods, what Lewis had liked most was the huge surrounding lawn, all covered with snow. But now that the snow had melted and he was in charge of mowing, he thought of the lawn as one big all-day job.

But the lawn was the very last thing on his mind this afternoon as he ran up onto the wide porch, skipping the last two steps. Unlocking the front door and turning the key in the new alarm system, Lewis charged into the house, broad-jumping onto the small hall rug and sliding across the floor into the kitchen. He threw his jacket in the general direction of the kitchen table and headed straight for the refrigerator. There was a note on the refrigerator door. *Remember the lawn.*

Lewis opened the door, grabbed the milk carton along with as many cookies as he could hold in his other hand, shut the door with his knee, and, with his teeth, pulled the note out from underneath the banana magnet. The refrigerator door was covered with magnets: strawberries, cherries, peaches, bunches of green grapes. A regular fruit salad.

Remember the lawn. Remember the Alamo, Lewis thought as he looked out the window at the lawn, which seemed to be growing larger by the minute. Maybe he could lower the blade on the mower so it would cut the grass all the way to the ground. That way he would only have to mow every two weeks. He'd have to work on that idea later. Today was a day for celebration, not for chores.

Lewis threw his mother's note, the cookie crumbs, and

his school notebook into the trash can and headed up to his bedroom.

His room, at the back of the house, had a ceiling that sloped down to a dormer with a big window. Before the alarm system was installed, Lewis could open that window and slide down onto the porch roof over the back door. Now, with the alarm in, Lewis had to go downstairs first and turn it off, taking all of the fun out of his escapes. "A small price to pay for security," his father had pointed out. "Especially since we'll be away all summer."

Having already switched off the alarm, Lewis now opened his bedroom window and slid out onto the small roof. At the edge he lowered himself down the drainpipe. He performed this trick only in the afternoon, when his parents weren't at home. He'd already broken off two of the brackets that held the pipe in place. "The stairs," his mother constantly reminded him, "are preferred."

Lewis ran across the yard and through the dense laurel bushes that bordered the woods and had served as the inspiration for their street's name, Laurelwood Road. On the other side of the bushes Lewis was in a dark, damp world of tall oaks and evergreens. There was little undergrowth because the sun rarely passed through the thick canopy of big trees.

Still running hard, Lewis swerved around a large rock, nicknamed "Stonehenge," and soon reached his favorite climbing tree, a thick oak with a tangle of strong branches, one of which grew low enough so that, with a good running start and a high jump, he could grab hold and swing himself up.

He climbed to the highest limb that would hold his weight. From there a cool wind blew through the trees and he could feel the branch swaying back and forth. Lewis could see over the tops of the trees to his house and, in the other direction, beyond the woods and across Route 22, to the big shopping center. Lewis's father had given him a terrific book about a sailor named Billy Budd, and today he pretended that he was Billy Budd, perched high atop the mast of a great sailing ship that was cutting smoothly through a calm sea. He kept a watch out for whales and for pirates. But when he saw his mother's car pulling into the driveway, he started down the mast.

Waiting for Lewis on the ground, with her spotted pink tongue hanging out and practically turning cartwheels with excitement, was Bunny, the ugly terrier that belonged to Lewis's across-the-street neighbors, the Ruperts. As far as Lewis was concerned, Bunny spent far too much time in the woods and certainly too much time in the Dees' yard, leaving behind her "chores," as Mrs. Rupert liked to call them. Lewis called them "mines." To step on one meant certain death. Some sections of his yard were so heavily mined that he had to avoid them altogether. Mowing was bad enough, but Bunny made it dangerous.

Lewis broke into a run as soon as his sneakered feet touched the ground, racing toward the house with Bunny in hot pursuit. As he ran through the laurel hedges, he saw Mrs. Rupert talking to his mother. Talking was Frances Rupert's favorite pastime, right up there with minding everybody else's business. Lewis wondered how Mr. Rupert could stand it. Between his wife's nonstop yakking and her ridiculous dog's nonstop yapping, life across the street at 12 Laurelwood Road must have been pretty noisy.

As Lewis ran up to the car, Mrs. Rupert was going on and on about something that had happened to her at the supermarket.

". . . and I told her, right to her face, that for a checkout girl at the A&P she certainly was acting uppity. I mean, did you ever see the girls they hire there? They couldn't get jobs anywhere else. The nerve of her!"

"Hi, Mom," Lewis managed to squeeze in.

"Hi, honey." Lewis's mother bent over and gave him a quick kiss. "Help me with the groceries, okay?"

"Hello, Lewis. Don't you have school today?" Mrs. Rupert asked him, but before he could answer she turned back to his mother. "So I went straight to the manager. I mean, am I going to waste my time arguing with some smart-aleck girl who probably dropped out of high school and is living with her boyfriend? Have you ever seen the makeup on those girls? And the hairdos they come up with. I'd be ashamed to be seen outdoors. . . ."

Lewis took the keys and opened the trunk. Two bags. When Lewis returned for the second one, Mrs. Rupert practically had his mother pinned against the hood of the Honda. He grabbed the bag, slammed the trunk closed, and came around to rescue her.

"Mom? C-c-could I talk to you, p-p-p-please?" *Look sincere,* Lewis told himself.

"Sure, honey. What is it?"

"In p-p-private." *Now go from sincere to upset,* he coached himself. Timing was crucial for the full effect. "In private" sounded kind of silly, but Mrs. Rupert would buy it, and if it got his mother away from Mrs. Motormouth, great.

"Oh, of course." His mother smiled. "Frances, would you excuse us?"

"Certainly, dear. I'll call you later. You just have to hear what that manager said to me. Talk about ignorant! You simply won't believe it. I told him that I'm writing to the president of the whole supermarket chain to complain."

"Nice talking to you," his mother said convincingly. What an actress, he thought. "Nice listening to you" would have been more like it.

"Sorry to hear about Bunny's condition," she added as she and Lewis walked up to the house. Mrs. Rupert half smiled and called to Bunny to accompany her home. But Bunny was far too busy watering the tires of the Honda.

"I hate that d-d-dog," Lewis whispered as they reached the front door.

"She's just a little high-strung," his mother said diplomatically.

"Yeah, well, I—I—I . . ."

"Take your time. Remember what Dr. Waldman said. Think of the word, see it in your head, and then just read it."

"I think that d-dog is n-n-nuts," he stuttered.

His mother laughed as they entered the kitchen together. "Funny you should say that. Frances was just telling me she's started taking Bunny to a dog psychologist."

They both laughed as they began unpacking the groceries. Then his mother stopped and turned to him.

"I spoke with Dr. Waldman today," she said.

Lewis waited.

"He's very excited with your progress, and he made an interesting suggestion." She paused. "There's this summer camp up near Lakeview. In the mountains. It has a full staff of speech therapists to work with the kids. He thought you would really like it up there. They have horseback riding. A beautiful lake. Tennis." Another long pause. "Lewis, you know how much your father and I love having you travel with us, and I know you're looking forward to the Arctic. But I want you to think seriously about this, okay? It could be a real help to you."

Lewis felt all prickly and hot. Camp? Oh, boy, no way. He couldn't go to a summer camp. Live in a cabin with other kids? New kids? New Stanley Flynns? School was bad enough. And what about the Arctic? And the polar bears? And the penguins?

Lewis's mother saw the horror on his face.

"This is a special camp," she assured him.

"S-s-s-special? With retards or s-s-something? I'm n-n-not re-tar-ded!"

"Lewis! It's not at all what you're thinking. Most of the kids have speech problems. Like you. Some have reading problems. The point is, they all have a good time together. And they help each other. There are camping trips and boating. It's supposed to be a beautiful camp. I want you to at least talk to Dr. Waldman about it. Okay? He has brochures with pictures and, well, he can explain it better than I can."

"Does Dad know about this c-c-c-camp?"

"I mentioned it to him. We talked about it."

"A-and w-w-what did he say?"

"He wants you to do what you want and what you think is best." Pause again. "Lewis, I don't want you to feel as if we're pushing you into this. But you've done so well with Dr. Waldman in the short time we've been here. Your father and I think you should take advantage of what this camp has to offer. Please think about it."

"What's the n-name of th-th-this c-camp?"

"Camp Chicopee."

Chicopee. What a dumb name. How would he ever pronounce that one without stuttering? "I'm going out back." Lewis turned and went out the kitchen door without another word.

IT WAS DARK when his father came out to get him for dinner. Lewis was so lost in thought that he hadn't even heard his car pull into the driveway. And he'd mowed not just half of the lawn but the whole thing. In fact, he'd started going over it again.

"Time for dinner, Lewis!" his father shouted over the

roar of the motor. Lewis turned it off and together they pushed it back to the shed.

"So, your mother told you about Camp Chicopee? What do you think?"

Lewis just shrugged.

"Your mother and I aren't forcing you, you know. Why don't you talk with Dr. Waldman and then we'll see." His father put his arm around him. "So, what do you say we eat? I'm starving."

Lewis knew that he wouldn't need to talk to Dr. Waldman or look at the camp brochures or discuss it with his parents. He already knew what was going to happen. He just hoped Camp Chicopee wouldn't be too bad.

2

A Little Fun

LEWIS'S PARENTS stood on the platform waving as the train pulled away. Watching them through the window, Lewis saw his mother reach quickly underneath her sunglasses with her hand—a swift wiping motion—and he felt sad, as if he missed them already. That, he decided, was impossible, for there they stood in their traveling clothes, his mother and father, growing smaller by the second. The incredible shrinking parents, he thought, watching until they were no more than tiny bright dots. Then the train rounded a curve and they vanished.

Lewis settled into his seat and watched the scenery speed by. He saw rows of neat little houses, their square backyards pushing up against high fences. In each yard he saw swing sets and barbecues, lawn furniture and green hoses coiled up like snakes. Little children in playsuits ran under sprinklers and splashed in wading pools.

Lewis thought of his parents, now on their way to the airport for their flight to Greenland, where they would meet the expedition ship that would take them to the Arctic. They were going to a place so remote that there wasn't even a post office. They wouldn't be able to write to Lewis all summer long.

Then he thought of all the trains he'd ridden on with them all over the world. English trains, with their first-class compartments, all red leather and starched fabrics and polished wood. India, where Lewis had gone with his father when he was only eight, had trains with cold hard seats. Black locomotive smoke poured in through windows that were so caked with soot, he and his father couldn't close them.

Lewis's reverie was interrupted when the train slowed down at the curve approaching the quarry, where a lot of kids went swimming. Of course, he thought of Stanley Flynn, and he actually had to stop himself from jumping out of his seat and running down the aisle. But then his fear was replaced by relief. Camp would be different. Or would it?

Lewis didn't have time to think about camp, for just then, as if by thinking something bad he had made it happen, Lewis looked out the window and saw them. Up ahead, running alongside the slowed train, were Stanley Flynn, Cycle, Wanker, and Cheese. Towels tied around their necks and their hair still wet from swimming, they were running, reaching up, grabbing hold, and pulling themselves on board.

Oh, no! Lewis slid down in his seat and hid his face in his comic book. Maybe they wouldn't see him. Maybe they wouldn't even come back to his car. Maybe they'd stay up front. Maybe they'd get caught. Sure. Fat chance. He was trapped.

Lewis glanced around the train car that was filled with strangers. No one to help him. His stomach churning, he desperately tried to read his comic book, a jungle adventure. Cartoon heroes didn't stutter, he thought. He closed his eyes and tried to picture himself in the comic-book jungle, cutting through the dense undergrowth with a machete on his way to rescue a beautiful girl or his best friend.

But he was rudely yanked out of his jungle paradise.

"Hey, L-L-L-Lewis Dee! What are you doing on this t-t-t-train? Running away from home?"

Lewis felt the blood rush to his face as he looked up into the leering face of Stanley Flynn. He struggled to speak. If only he could say something, stand up to Flynn just once, but the words stuck hard in his throat. His heart began pounding so loudly that he was sure Flynn must be able to hear it.

"What's wrong, L-L-L-Lewis? Cat got your tongue?" Flynn roared at his own joke as if it were the funniest thing in the world.

The conductor's voice crackled over the loudspeaker. "Sayerville. Sayerville. All departing passengers please check the overhead racks for your belongings. Sayerville next."

The door at the end of the car opened and Cycle strutted in, followed by the rest of Flynn's crew—each one uglier and meaner than the last.

"Hey, guys!" Flynn yelled. "Come on back here. Looks like we're riding in the circus car with the freaks."

Cheese spotted him. "Check it out, guys," he shouted, pointing right at Lewis. "It's the c-c-c-creep himself."

It seemed to Lewis as if everyone in the car was looking. As a matter of fact, everyone was looking. But no one came to help, and then, as if they all were watching a television program they didn't want to see, at exactly the same time they turned back to their newspapers and magazines and conversations.

"Sayerville. Sayerville," the conductor's voice boomed. The train slowed down as Cycle, Wanker, and Cheese gathered around Flynn for their own version of "a little fun." Sayerville wasn't the camp stop, not even close, but Lewis suddenly knew that it was going to be his stop.

He didn't have much time. He jumped up and grabbed

his duffel bag from the overhead rack. The train jerked to a stop, throwing Lewis off balance and catapulting his bag through the air. It hit Flynn right in the face with an ominous thud.

"Yeow!" Flynn yelled, recoiling in pain and covering his face with his hands.

Lewis's brand-new heavy-duty flashlight, tucked away in the end pocket of the duffel bag, had just justified its high price. Lewis figured that Flynn would have a whopper of a black eye, but there was no time to wait and see. He pushed his way through Flynn's stunned friends, grabbed his bag, and ran down the aisle. The doors slid open with a hiss, and Lewis ran out.

Across the platform and down the staircase, he kept running, dragging his heavy duffel bag, until he heard the doors slide shut and the train lurch to a start. Then he turned and looked. Through the windows he could see Stanley Flynn, still bent over with his head in his hands and his friends surrounding him. The train picked up speed and they all disappeared. Just like that.

SAYERVILLE. Sayerville? Lewis looked around. There was no one on the platform. The parking lot was empty. He could feel the hot sun warming his back as he stood alone by the tracks. He'd left his comic book on the train seat, and he couldn't help thinking about what those guys would do to it when they found it.

What he really had to think about, however, was what he was going to do now. Where was Sayerville, anyhow? Lewis stared into the distance, and the train tracks seemed to stretch out ahead of him like the long, empty summer vacation. He turned and walked up to the station window. There was a schedule posted there. He'd have to catch the next train north. To summer camp.

3

A Black Hole in Space

LEWIS SIGHED WITH RELIEF as he turned the corner onto Laurelwood Road and the long white porch of his house came into view. The house looked so quiet and safe, like a castle surrounded by its moat of lawn.

Sitting down on his duffel bag in the fading daylight, he counted his money. Enough for another train ticket and a little left over for food. When he ran off the train, Lewis hadn't stopped to consider the possibility that there might not be another train north from Sayerville that day. He was lucky there'd been a train back to North Renfield, otherwise he would have really been stuck.

He sat there, staring at his house, thinking about his parents, who were on their way to Greenland now, assuming that he was safe at camp. And that's when it dawned on him. He didn't want to go to camp. And his parents already thought he was at camp. So why not just stay home for the next eight weeks? Who would know? No one, that's who. Sure, he'd have to sneak around, he couldn't be seen by the neighbors. But one thing was for sure. He wouldn't have to talk to another person for practically the entire summer!

Lewis jumped up, grabbed his bag, and ducked into the woods. He had to get into the house without being seen and without setting off the alarm. He had no house keys with him, so the doors were out. But there was a way.

He stood just inside the darkness of the woods. The Ruperts' curtains were drawn shut. He took a deep breath, imagined that he was an Olympic sprinter going for the gold, and ran across the open space between the woods and the house. When he reached the front porch, he threw his bag underneath and then followed, sliding into the darkness. He peeked out and looked across the street. All clear.

Dragging his duffel bag, he crawled through the damp dirt along the length of the porch. The family who had owned the house before the Dees had had the porch extended, and in doing so had covered up a basement window —a window that was not hooked up to the new alarm system. Lewis had discovered it one day while exploring in the basement. It was a small window, built into the stone foundation. With a little help from his belt buckle it opened easily.

Lewis threw his bag in and then, feet first, followed, dropping down into total darkness. It wasn't going to be easy to make his way through the basement. He couldn't see anything, including the door in the wall that divided the basement in two. He held a finger up in front of his nose, and he couldn't even see that. Running a hand along the rough stone wall, he felt caked dirt, damp cracks, and all kinds of gucky things. It gave him the willies.

Maybe there were bugs or rats or even snakes down there, and he might accidentally touch one, Lewis thought, his imagination running wild. With his hands out in front of him to protect his face, Lewis shuffled through the dark, one step at a time. Maybe he should sing or make noise or something? No. He didn't want to attract any unnecessary attention in case a bat was trying to find him. A bat! Oh, boy, why did he have to think of that?

It seemed to take forever to cross the room, but he finally reached the light switch and flipped it on. There was a brief burst of light and then it was dark again. The bulb had burned out!

Now, don't panic, Lewis told himself over and over, repeating it like the Indian mantra his mother chanted when she was doing her yoga exercises. Feeling carefully with his hands, he opened the heavy door to the main room of the basement. If possible, that room seemed even darker. The stairs that led up to the kitchen and the switch for the overhead light were clear across the room. A black hole in space. A hole filled with every imaginable object, from Lewis's bicycle to an old canoe to stacks of magazines.

Well, he figured he had eight weeks to cross the room, so he pointed himself in what he hoped was the right direction and started walking. Suddenly he remembered his brand-new flashlight! The very flashlight that had rescued him from the wrath of Flynn was tucked away in his duffel bag, back below the window. Great. Swell. How could he be so stupid? That brand-new flashlight was just sitting there. Brand-new batteries. All ready to go. Guaranteed to light up one thousand square feet. Even underwater.

WHEN LEWIS FINALLY FELT the cool metal of the clothes washer and dryer, he knew that he had reached his goal. He swept his hand along the wall, searching for the light switch.

Lights! The fluorescent light blinded Lewis when he looked right into it. There was only one problem: He hadn't found the switch yet. The light had come on by itself!

Someone had flipped on the switch upstairs. Uh-oh. Someone else was in the house!

"M-M-M-Mom? D-Dad?" Lewis called out tentatively, his voice pitched about five octaves above normal.

No answer. Lewis looked around for a place to hide and for a weapon.

"M-M-Mom?" he called again, all the while knowing that his parents were on their way to Greenland. He held his breath and listened. Not a sound. Lewis looked up at the light and desperately came up with a plan.

"D-D-Dad?" he managed to squeak out one last time. Nothing. He didn't waste another second. He took a hard look at the path back to the furnace room, then switched off the light. Darkness. He swung around and charged toward the door, praying that he was on the path he'd mapped out in his mind.

He wasn't. The canoe was stored upside down on two sawhorses. When he ran into it, it not only stopped him dead in his tracks, it also knocked the wind out of him. Lewis landed on the floor, gasping for air. He rolled over on his side and knocked over his bicycle, which fell on top of him. And then the light came back on again! He pushed the bicycle away and crawled away on his hands and knees as fast as he could, hiding behind a stack of empty cartons that their appliances had come in. There was the box for the stereo. One for the big fan. The air conditioner. The television. The box from the light timer system. The timer. The light timer!

Lewis leaned against the wall and cried and laughed at the same time. The timer was hooked up to lights all over the house so that it would look from the outside as if someone was at home all summer. Well, Lewis decided, if the timer didn't keep burglars away, it sure would scare them to death once they got inside.

4

Lewis Is Alone

THE PHONE CONVERSATION with the camp director wasn't easy for Lewis because of his stutter, which was always much worse when he was nervous and when he was talking to an adult. And especially when he was lying. But he was able to get across the fact that he wasn't coming to camp after all and that he'd be traveling with his parents instead. The director requested a formal letter from Lewis's father as soon as possible, wished Lewis a good summer, and hung up. Done. Lewis stood for a minute with the receiver in his hand, listening to the dial tone, realizing that that conversation might have been the last one he'd have for eight weeks. Then he went right upstairs to his computer and typed out a short letter to the director, printing it on his father's stationery. It was pretty convincing, he thought, especially the signature, which, like his father's, was completely illegible, just a bunch of squiggles.

Then Lewis moved on to the next most important subject —his stomach. There was nothing in the refrigerator. In fact, it was shut off. The cupboards in the pantry, usually packed with canned goods and boxes of food, were almost empty. Lewis took an inventory, putting everything on one shelf. There was a six-pack of beer (he didn't drink), two cans of tomato paste, a box of noodles, a can of peas (yuck), six packets of yeast, a two-pound box of dried milk, and one can of mandarin oranges. How depressing. Things didn't look too bright in the food department. Lewis ate the oranges right out of the can and then, still hungry, he ate the peas, something he never did.

Finally, Lewis lay down to sleep, in his own bed at first, but that didn't work. An eerie light poured into his room from the full moon outside. Now that it was night, it was scary being in the house all alone. So he headed for his parents' room. He climbed into their big bed and buried his face in the blankets. He could smell his mother's perfume. Lewis inhaled deeply, waiting for sleep to come.

But he heard noises. House noises. Pipes were clanging, electrical appliances hummed, the walls creaked and groaned. Windows rattled in the summer wind. Lewis was wide awake. He couldn't even close his eyes. So he took the sheet from his parents' bed and started carefully down the stairs. On the landing between floors he stopped and sat, wrapped in the white sheet, keeping watch over the living room, looking like some odd, fidgety ghost.

When he got tired of sitting, Lewis slid down the carpeted staircase into the living room, working his way around the downstairs, trying out all possible sleeping spots. But he just couldn't get to sleep. He kept seeing shapes forming in the dark, sweeping across the room like night demons. They surrounded him, peered down curiously, as if they were wondering, who was this boy and why was he sleeping down here in the living room? Why was he alone in this big house? Where were his parents? Lewis wanted to run and hide, but he had no place to go. And no one to go to.

Finally, he curled up underneath the dining-room table, safe at last, protected by the low wooden roof over his head and the four table legs that kept out the night.

AFTER THE INITIAL SHOCK of waking up under the table the next morning, Lewis began to enjoy his adventure. He didn't have to talk to anyone. In fact, he couldn't talk even if he wanted to because there was no one to talk to. He was hiding out, living a secret life, and he might not have to talk for weeks.

He was just about to open the kitchen curtains to let in the sunlight when he heard Frances Rupert outside in the street talking to Bunny. Lewis ducked down fast.

"Bunny, sweetheart. Come to Mommy. Come on, baby," he heard her say.

That was a close one. He'd almost blown it on his very first morning. Rule Number One: Don't open any curtains facing the street.

So, in the muted morning light, Lewis went about preparing his breakfast, which took about a minute, since it was only noodles and salt. He had visions of sliced bananas and peaches on cereal. He was going to have to go food shopping that very day. No way he was eating yeast for lunch. Still hungry, he took another long look through the kitchen for something edible he might have missed, but there wasn't a thing. He mixed up a glass of powdered milk. It tasted like medicine.

Lewis raided his Statue of Liberty bank, his Space Shuttle bank, his penny collection, his father's top dresser drawer, his mother's change jar in the kitchen, and when he was done, he sat down at the kitchen table and counted. A grand total of forty-two dollars and fifty-five cents. Not so good, but enough to get him through the first few weeks, he guessed. It was clearly a guess, because he had no idea how much groceries cost. Boy, not only was school a bore, but they didn't teach you anything useful. He had a lot of things to learn.

It was too risky to go out during the day, Lewis realized. So, hungry as he was, his shopping trip would have to wait until dark. He occupied himself exploring the drawers and closets all through the house. In his father's closet he found an old hat that belonged to his grandfather. He put it on and, with a cigar he found in his father's desk, pretended that he was a gangster and that the house was surrounded by the police. The imaginary police chief, holding a megaphone, yelled from outside, "We've got you surrounded. Come out with your hands up or we're coming in after you!"

"N-n-no way. You'll never take me alive, c-coppers," Lewis shouted back in a thick voice. Shots were exchanged. He rummaged through the kitchen cabinets in search of extra ammunition.

It was hours before the police and the FBI finally stormed the house, cornering Lewis in his bedroom and filling him full of hot lead. He died a very dramatic death, falling from his bed to the floor. Then he put the hat and the cigar back. It was getting dark. Time to sneak out to the supermarket.

Lewis made his way down through the basement and the furnace room and out the little window. He dashed across the backyard, his pants full of loose change that jangled in his pockets. When he was safe inside the dark woods he rested for a minute, and then made his way to the shopping center.

5

Sneaky Mrs. Rupert

FRANCES RUPERT was out for her evening stroll with Bunny. As was her habit, she walked down the center of the road, enjoying the night air, calling out to her beloved dog until, out of sight of her house and her husband, she purposefully veered off toward the edge of the woods, calling softly to Bunny to follow.

Hidden from prying eyes, she walked with determination to a large rock at the base of an evergreen tree, and there she bent down and picked up a small metal box. Opening it, she sighed as she took out a pack of cigarettes. Mrs. Rupert's one sin was her nightly cigarette. She felt positively wicked when she was smoking. Her husband would have a fit if he knew, since they both had supposedly given up the nasty habit. But just one a day couldn't possibly hurt her, she reasoned, and besides, she was quite proud of herself for being so clever about it. Seating herself daintily on the rock, she lit up, took a deep drag, and sighed again, this time even louder and with more pleasure. Then she puffed away.

That's just where Lewis saw her on his way back from his first shopping trip, trudging along through the woods with two heavy grocery bags. As he stopped to rest, sitting on the spongy pine-needle-carpeted forest floor, he proudly examined his purchases: SpaghettiOs; peanut butter and jelly; crackers; English muffins; frozen waffles; frozen pizza; ice cream; chocolate syrup; milk; canned soups and fruits and tuna fish; lots of soda pop. He'd spent almost all of his money, but tonight he wasn't going to worry about that. Tonight he was happy. He had gone an entire day without having to talk to anyone even once. And now there was a nice breeze and the moon was almost full and the woods were quiet except for—uh-oh! Lewis ducked down when he saw the small flame shoot up. A match. In its brief light he recognized Frances Rupert. And there was Bunny, jumping up and down and licking Lewis's face while he tried desperately to calm the crazed animal.

Soon Mrs. Rupert was finished with her cigarette. Ever so careful about forest fires, she snuffed the butt out in the metal box and tucked it back into its hiding place between the rock and the tree. She called out softly to Bunny. But Bunny was too busy with Lewis to hear her. So she called more loudly, and when that didn't work, she began to threaten.

"Bunny Rupert, you come out of there this instant, you naughty dog, or you're going to be punished! Mommy is getting angry. Do you hear me?"

No response. Then Mrs. Rupert threatened to come in after her and give her "a good wallop!" She stood at the edge of the woods, tapping her foot while she sucked on a breath mint and rubbed her hands with pine needles to get rid of the cigarette smell. In desperation Lewis took a can of tuna from one of his bags and whacked the little beast on the nose. Bunny let out a yelp and ran from the woods right into the arms of her mistress, whining and whimpering all the way.

"Baby doll, what is it? What's wrong?" Mrs. Rupert asked, waiting as if she actually expected an answer. She squinted and tried to see into the woods, nervously backing away at the same time. Something in there had frightened her brave Bunny. Did she see something? She wasn't sure. Finally she turned and hurried back up the street to the safety of her house and her husband.

Lewis waited until the coast was clear and then carried his grocery bags home. Peanut butter and jelly had never tasted so good.

6

The Crazy Camper

LEWIS STOOD BY HIS BEDROOM WINDOW and waited for the sun to set. Nearly two weeks had gone by, and he had settled into a routine of sleeping during the day and staying up a good part of the night. He was almost out of all the food he'd bought, and with only seven dollars left, what would he eat for the next six weeks? Maybe he'd have to pick through the neighbors' garbage cans. That didn't sound too appetizing, but it was better than stealing from the grocery store. It would be easy enough, since he'd been sneaking his garbage into his neighbors' cans for the last two weeks.

Even though he'd decided not to use any of the doors in the house, Lewis shut off the alarm system so he could use his favorite escape route. And now that it was dark, he opened his bedroom window, slid across the back porch roof, and down the drainpipe to the ground.

The woods at night were a whole different world. He could go for hours just trying to catch fireflies, their little lights winking on and off as they darted about, up and down, in and out of the trees. He had to make quick guesses as to which direction they were headed, so when their lights blinked on he'd grab a little ahead and, wham, he'd get one.

Tonight, however, the fireflies were safe from Lewis. He had other more important things to do. He had worked diligently all week on an elaborate treasure map, and tonight was the night to test it out. A final check to make sure that there were no mistakes and that the map could be followed.

Lewis traced the map's arrows and dotted line through the laurel bushes, thirty-five paces north by northeast. He had, of course, brought his compass along. He stood on the fallen log, jumped as far as he could due west, turned to the south, and walked forty paces until he came to Stonehenge.

As he walked off those paces, he noticed a small moving light that grew as he drew nearer. Lewis stuffed his treasure map into his back pocket. If it was a firefly, it certainly was the biggest one he had ever seen. He tiptoed along carefully, working on a plan to capture this monster bug. Just as Lewis was wondering if big fireflies could bite, his Godzilla firefly dropped to the ground and began to cough and retch. Lewis ducked behind a tree. Someone was in the woods!

Maybe it was just Mrs. Rupert sneaking another cigarette, but what was she doing so deep in the woods? And where was her faithful companion, Bunny? Lewis decided to climb the tree for a better look. Slowly, pretending he was a panther, he made his way up and shimmied out on a branch for a good view. It wasn't Frances Rupert. It was difficult to be sure in the dark, but it looked like a boy about his own age who had set up a camp. There was a sleeping bag and a pup tent and a backpack. Food cans and pots and paper plates were scattered on the ground. Whoever he was, he'd been trying to smoke a cigarette, obviously without much success. That meant it wasn't anyone from Flynn's gang, since they were all accomplished smokers.

Lewis leaned farther out on the branch. This guy looked fat. And from up above it sounded as if he was talking to himself. Uh-oh. Maybe there were two of them. He crawled out even farther, trying to hear what the fat boy was saying.

Crack! The branch snapped off the tree, and Lewis, holding on tight, plummeted to the earth. He landed with a nasty thud, still clutching the branch. The next thing he heard was the mysterious boy tripping over his own camping gear as he ran away, yelling, "Wild animals!" into the night.

Lewis reluctantly let go of the branch and tried to move each of his own limbs. Good. Nothing broken. In fact, nothing even hurt much. He looked way up into the tree from which he had fallen and couldn't help but let out a nervous laugh. Standing up slowly, he brushed the dirt from his clothes. The boy was nowhere to be seen, so Lewis sneaked over to inspect his camp.

It was all very strange. First of all, the pup tent was painted with crazy symbols of the sun and the moon, like some Indian tepee. And the food! There were cans of food that Lewis had never heard of, let alone eaten. Artichoke hearts. Marinated smoked oysters. Duck-liver pâté. And something completely bizarre in mustard sauce that he couldn't even come close to pronouncing. Well, whoever this boy was, he wasn't going to get very far without his flashlight, which he'd left lying next to his deflated air mattress. This guy liked to travel in comfort, Lewis figured, picking up a battery-operated fan. He turned to the backpack. Maybe there was some clue inside. But just as he opened the top flap, there was a blood-curdling scream and the boy came charging out of the darkness, waving his arms like a madman. As he lunged at Lewis, he tripped over one of the tent pegs and fell flat on his face, grabbing one of Lewis's legs and pulling him down right on top of the tent.

Terrified, Lewis yanked his leg free, jumped up, and,

without a backward look, ran all the way through the woods to his house.

IT WAS VERY EARLY the next morning when Lewis lowered himself down the drainpipe. Another clamp that held the pipe to the house was about to pull loose. That meant he was going to have to find a new escape route. The grass was still wet with dew, and soon his sneakers were soaked. It was early, but Frances Rupert would be walking her ridiculous dog soon, so Lewis knew he had to work fast. Last night, when he'd realized that his treasure map was missing, it was all he could do to stop himself from going back to look for it right then. He didn't want to risk being seen, but the sooner he found the map, the better he'd feel. That boy, if he found it first, might dig up the treasure and steal it.

As he walked in the forest, it seemed as if every sound he made was magnified. He was sure he'd wake up the sleeping boy. When he got within twenty feet of the campsite, he got down on his hands and knees, crawled behind a tree, and cautiously looked out. The pup tent was collapsed on one side where Lewis had landed on it the night before. The backpack was missing, but he figured it was probably inside the tent. That's where the map would be if this guy had indeed found it. Lewis hoped that the crazy camper was still asleep. He'd need a little time.

It had been so dark the night before that chances were good that the map was just lying on the ground somewhere. Slowly Lewis crept up to the camp. No map in sight. It seemed awfully quiet. Maybe this guy was already on the trail with the treasure map. Lewis crawled over to the tree he'd fallen from. The broken branch was still there, but no map. He was getting worried. Would he actually have to fight this guy to get his map back?

Suddenly the tent swayed from side to side like a lumbering animal. He was awake! Lewis leapt up into the tree and climbed around to the far side so that the trunk hid him from view. Then he peeked around to watch.

The boy crawled out of the tent and looked around with sleepy eyes. His face was all puffed up, and his round stomach stuck out between his T-shirt and his shorts. He stood up, yawned, stretched, then scratched himself all over—he was covered with mosquito bites—until his arms and legs and neck were bright red.

Lewis got a good look at him in the daylight. He was about Lewis's age, maybe a little older, but Lewis had never seen him around town. Maybe he was a runaway.

Lewis began to feel sorry for him. He looked so uncomfortable, all hunched over, mumbling to himself, scratching his bites. The boy picked up one of the food cans and bashed it against a rock. Then he put the can on the ground, picked up another rock, and bashed it against the can. After he'd pounded the can every possible way and it still wouldn't open, he picked it up and threw it off into the woods. "I hope the crocodile eats you!" he yelled.

Crocodile? There weren't any crocodiles in upstate New York. Not that Lewis knew of, anyway. This guy was getting weirder by the minute.

Pulling a stack of papers from the tent, he started reading aloud. Lewis listened hard but could only pick up an occasional word. "Pirates." "Indians." Something about "flying" and "lost boys." Lost boys? Maybe he really was a runaway. Then he cleared his throat very loudly, made some funny sounds as if he was testing his voice, and he started to sing. Lewis was amazed. He wondered if this guy had speech problems too. Why was he singing and doing those weird voice exercises?

Lewis completely forgot about his treasure map.

Then he saw it. They both saw it at the same time. One corner of the yellow paper was sticking out from underneath the tent. How could he have missed it? Lewis wondered, as he watched the boy pick it up.

"Oh, wow. Pirate city," the boy said. "This must belong to Captain Hook. All right!"

Before he could stop himself, Lewis yelled out, "T-t-that's m-my m-m-m-map."

The boy spun around and looked up at him.

"Oh, wow. Like, major invasion of privacy," he said. "Why don't you, like, remove yourself from that tree before you do the old 'bombs away' routine again?"

"No," Lewis said.

"What do you mean, no? How do you think you're going to get your map back?" the boy asked.

"Are you a r-r-r-r . . ." Lewis stuttered.

"A what?"

"A r-r-runaway?" Lewis asked him.

"I'm a Lost Boy, that's what I am," he said, waving the map in the air. "Now, how long are you going to stay up there in bird city?"

A lost boy? He didn't look lost.

Lewis started to work his way down the tree. This guy sure was strange, but Lewis figured he could easily outrun him if it came to that. And, who knew, maybe he was all right.

"I'm Max Winkler," the boy said when Lewis reached the ground. He put out his hand and Lewis shook it.

"I'm Lewis."

"I ought to rearrange your face, Lewis, for spying on me last night."

Lewis put a hand up to block the expected punch. But it didn't come.

"Hey, relax, squirrel man. I'm not going to hit you. I

just want to know why you were spying on me. I ain't bothering you."

"I came back for m-m-m—"

"Your map?" Max interrupted. "Hey, you stutter or something?"

Lewis nodded and looked down at his feet. He hated this part of it. Whenever he first met someone, it was as if the words were locked up inside, and with them the chance for friendship.

"Here's your map." Max broke the silence, handing him the treasure map. "Listen, you wouldn't happen to have a can opener on you, would you? I sort of forgot mine and I'm getting awfully hungry."

Lewis folded up the map and put it in his back pocket. "You c-c-can come to my h-house and—"

"Ah, no. I, um, can't. You see, I can't go to anyone's house. Can't you bring it here?"

"Why can't y-you c-c-c-come to my house?"

"I just can't," Max insisted. "You see, it's this, well, it's part of my preparation."

"What?" Lewis asked.

"Preparation. That's actor's lingo. It means getting ready for a role. You know." Max started to scratch his mosquito bites again. "Oh, glory, I'm covered with bites. Mosquito overload!"

"I'll get a c-c-can opener," Lewis said, and he turned and ran off before he burst out laughing. What a funny guy this Max was.

It wasn't until he reached his house and was climbing up to the porch roof that Lewis realized what had happened. Max was the first person he'd talked to in more than two weeks!

Lewis got the can opener from the kitchen and climbed out of the house. He hurried back into the woods. For the first time in his life he had to admit that it felt good to talk to someone. Or, at least, to try to talk.

"Here's the c-can opener. And I b-b-brought you this road map," he said as he approached the campsite. Max was sitting on his air mattress outside of the tent, spraying the air around him with insect repellent. His portable fan was going full blast.

"A road map?"

"You said you were l-l-lost," Lewis explained.

Max took the can opener and quickly went to work, lining up all of his cans of food and opening one after another. "Look, here's the real scoop: I'm not lost. I'm a Lost Boy. I have no parents, and I'm having an incredible adventure here, waiting for Peter to come back." Max took a spoon out of his backpack and went to work on the cans. Starting at one end of the line, he ate a spoonful from each one. When he reached the end of the line, he started back in the other direction.

Now Lewis was totally confused. For someone in Max's situation he seemed awfully calm. And who was Peter?

"You see," Max explained between spoonfuls, "when I was just a little baby, a few days old, I was lying in my crib and I heard my parents talking about what I was going to be when I grew up. My father said a lawyer. A lawyer! I almost gagged. So when they weren't looking, I jumped out of my crib and I crawled away."

"W-w-wh . . ." Lewis stuttered.

"Come on. You can do it," Max encouraged him.

"What!" Lewis blurted out.

"What what?"

Lewis always seemed to be confusing people with his stutter. He couldn't carry on a normal conversation with anyone. He'd gotten his treasure map back. Maybe he should just go home now.

"I'm s-s-sorry," Lewis said.

"Sorry? For what?"

Lewis just looked away.

"You bothered by your stutter?" Max held out one of the open cans and his spoon.

Lewis took them. He didn't know what was in the can, but he ate it anyway. Even when it was in his mouth, he couldn't figure out what it was. But he swallowed it anyway and smiled.

"Look, don't worry about it," Max assured him. "I've got a great idea. I'll do all of the talking and you can listen. How about that?"

Lewis smiled again.

"Look, I was sort of pulling your leg before. Like, uh, white-lie city. You dig?"

Lewis shook his head.

"See, I'm not really lost or anything. I'm an actor." He puffed up his chest. "In fact, I've often been told that I'm like a young Tom Cruise."

Max didn't look anything like Tom Cruise.

"Well, a young, slightly overweight Tom Cruise," Max admitted. "I mean, the way I see it, the only thing standing between me and superstardom is about fifteen pounds. Once I take care of that little problem—Hollywood, here I come!"

Fascinated, Lewis sat down on the ground. Max kept right on talking, about all kinds of things, making Lewis laugh as he jumped around, acting out his stories. Using different voices for different characters, Max actually put on a show. Maybe he really was headed for Hollywood, Lewis decided.

Max lived in New York City with his mother, an aspiring nightclub singer, and Lewis especially liked his stories about her. He did an impression of her nightclub act that had Lewis rolling on the ground. Then he told stories of the tough guys in his East Village neighborhood, and he demonstrated a couple of karate moves. "I usually joke my way out of trouble, but in the big N-Y-C, you can't be too careful." Lewis wasn't sure whether he was being serious or not. "On the street, things can turn ugly in a second," he said, snapping his fingers.

Lewis was tempted to tell his Detroit story, but Max launched right into another story without taking a breath.

"My parents are divorced, you know."

Lewis didn't know, but he nodded anyway.

"Yeah, three years now. They did the splitsville routine when I was ten. They just couldn't hack it together. My dad lives here in town. He's a psychology professor at the college."

Max became quiet, studying the label on one of the cans. Lewis didn't know what to say, so he watched him and waited. Finally Max started to talk again, just as fast as before, filling Lewis in on his present circumstances.

Max had just been been cast as one of the Lost Boys in the local summer theater production of *Peter Pan.* This was the second summer he'd spent working with the theater. Last summer he'd played the Artful Dodger in *Oliver!*, which, he assured Lewis, was "the most important role in the show." Max was so excited about being an actor, he'd already written an acceptance speech for his Academy Award.

"Hey, you never know, right?" Max rubbed his belly and sighed. "My ma might even come up to see the show this year." Then he changed the subject. "So, where'd you get the treasure map?"

"It's m-m-m-mine," Lewis told him.

"Sure, it's yours. I know that. But where'd you get it?"

"I m-made it."

"Yeah? No kidding? Let's see." Max held out his hand.

Lewis hesitated.

"Hey, what's the problem? Don't you trust me?" Max wanted to know.

Lewis took the map from his pocket and held it out.

"Look, buddy, if you don't trust me . . ." Max said.

"I t-t-trust you."

Max smiled and took the map. It was an impressive piece of work. Before Lewis had started drawing it, he'd soaked the paper in water and let it dry in the sun so that it got crinkled and yellow, like very old paper. Then he'd spent a full day working on it, using lots of different-colored pencils. When he was done, he burned the edges with a match to make it look like parchment.

Max whistled. "A very pro job, Lewis. I'm humbled, my friend. But tell me, what did you bury?"

"Stuff," Lewis said. "You want to see if you can f-f-find it?"

"For sure. Yeah. I can dig doing a Harrison Ford."

"What?" Lewis asked.

"Like *Raiders of the Lost Ark,* you know?" Max said, scratching at his bare arms and legs. "Now, where do I start? There gonna be any venomous snakes and horrible spiders and gorgeous women along the trail?"

Lewis laughed. "You want to f-f-finish your l-lunch first?"

"Great idea. It's hunger city here," Max said, patting his belly. It didn't take long for him to finish off what was left in the cans.

"You sure eat f-f-fast," Lewis said.

"Do I really?" Max smiled as he put the empty cans in a grocery bag. "I didn't even notice. I must have been famished." He was still scratching, and his body was covered with rashes and welts. He took a pair of long pants from the sagging tent and slipped them on over his shorts. He stuck his feet into a pair of sneakers without bothering to lace them up. His hair was sticking out in every direction. He looked like a punk rock star.

Lewis helped him clean up the campsite, and then, leaving Max alone to study the map, he ran home to get a shovel from the shed.

Lewis watched from behind the laurel hedge as Frances Rupert walked down the street with her rodentlike dog. He waited until she was out of sight and ran to the shed. He grabbed the shovel and dashed back into the woods while the coast was still clear.

When he found Max, he was nearly halfway through the map. Pretty good for twenty minutes, Lewis thought. In fact, he was a little upset. He had hoped it would be tougher than that. He'd have to make some adjustments in the map.

But the second half was more difficult to decipher. Max kept begging for hints, but Lewis wasn't about to help him. It was too much fun watching him struggle.

An hour later, after many miscalculations and wrong turns and what seemed like miles and miles of pacing, Max was finally ready to dig. "This is the spot," he announced, standing over a flat, star-shaped rock that sat all alone on a thick blanket of pine needles. He looked at Lewis, but Lewis just shrugged and handed him the shovel.

Lewis sat down against a tree and tried to look bored. It was the spot, and after only a few minutes the shovel hit the top of the wooden treasure box.

Max looked over at Lewis and a smile of victory spread across his face, from mosquito bite to mosquito bite. "Aha! I've found your priceless treasure," he said dramatically, posing with the shovel in his hand like a famous explorer.

Max dug carefully around the box and then lifted it out of the hole. "Is it booby-trapped?" he asked as he gingerly opened the lid. Inside were a bag of marbles, two silver dollars, a string of beads from Africa, coins from all over the world, Lewis's prize baseball cards, and three of his most valuable comic books.

"So I get to keep all this stuff, right?" Max asked.

"No w-w-way," Lewis said.

"Just kidding, buddy. Just kidding."

After Lewis explained the importance of each item, the boys placed the box in the hole and filled it back up with dirt. They patted the earth down carefully, adding a layer of leaves and pine needles to make it look natural. Then they placed the star-shaped rock on top. Lewis wiped out their footprints around the area with a branch. "You can never be t-t-too careful about these things," he said.

"Yeah. You never know when someone might be camping around here," Max said. They both laughed.

LEWIS SPENT THE REST of the afternoon showing his new friend around the woods, which Max dubbed "the northern end of Never-Never Land." He showed Max his favorite climbing tree. Since Max was from New York City, he had never climbed a tree. Lewis gave him his first lesson. Max was eager to learn, but he decided not to climb beyond the lower, thicker branches. "There's always the possibility of falling, as you well know," he reminded Lewis. "I'd better stay down here and keep a lookout for Indians and pirates."

Eventually the boys made their way to the steep embankment leading up to the highway that separated the woods from the shopping center. Max started to complain about being hungry again.

"It's not really good to be this hungry," he said with great seriousness. "It could make you sick." His eyes were filled with longing as he looked across the highway at the golden arches that beckoned from the shopping center. "Perhaps we could slip across the road and have a quick snack.

Just some fries," he said. "A couple of cheeseburgers. A milk shake. Some of those chicken things with dip."

"What about your preparation?" Lewis reminded him. "You're not supposed to leave the woods, right?"

Max frowned. "Becoming an actor is tough work," he admitted as they climbed down the embankment. The golden arches disappeared from view. "I wonder if Tom Cruise ever has to go hungry?"

The afternoon sun cut through the trees as the two boys made their way back to the campsite. Max hummed a song the whole way back.

As they tried to straighten the lopsided tent, which was sagging even worse than before, Max talked constantly about food. Lewis was pretty hungry too. He hadn't eaten anything since early that morning. And there was very little left of the food he'd bought on his shopping trip weeks before. They searched through Max's backpack for a possible forgotten can, but there was none left.

"They say certain parts of pine trees are edible. What do you think?" Max asked, picking at a piece of bark.

"I've got a b-b-better idea," Lewis said. "I'll g-go home and g-get some food and bring it b-b-b-back here." That way, they could eat without Max leaving the woods and breaking his rule. Max loved the idea.

"Bring a lot!" he yelled as Lewis ran off to his house. "And something to drink. And dessert. Don't forget dessert!" He lay down on his air mattress and fell asleep.

Back in his kitchen Lewis took a grocery bag and filled it with all the food that was left. He grabbed a quart of soda pop and made his way down to the basement. The under-the-porch escape route would be easier than having to carry the bag down the drainpipe, he figured. Plus he could get a view of the street before crossing his backyard. He had to make sure that the coast was clear.

Lewis hummed the theme song from *Superman* as he crawled out from under the porch. Hugging the grocery bag in one arm and cradling the soda bottle under the other like a football, he shot across the yard. Halfway to the woods he heard Bunny bark, but Lewis just kept going. He made it to the laurel hedge, then, safely hidden, he turned to see if he'd been spotted. He expected to see Bunny bounding across his backyard with Mrs. Rupert following close behind. Nope. No Bunny. No Mrs. Rupert either. Bunny was tied up in the Ruperts' front yard, yapping away at a neighborhood cat.

LEWIS AND MAX STUFFED THEMSELVES as Max talked about acting. He showed Lewis his script and songbook from *Peter Pan,* and he told him the story of the Lost Boys and how they lived together in Never-Never Land with Peter Pan as their leader. With his mouth full of peanut butter and crackers he sang a couple of the songs. Soon Lewis found himself singing along.

"Hey, you're pretty good," Max said. "Why don't you come and try out for one of the Lost Boys? They need some more kids and it'd be great. You and me, man. We'd knock 'em dead. Forget *Cats.* Forget *A Chorus Line.* It'd be *The Max and Lewis Show.* Wow!"

"I can't," Lewis told him, even though he wished more than anything that he could.

"You can't? Why not? Your parents won't let you?"

"No. I c-c-can't act. I st-st-stutter too m-much."

"But you didn't stutter at all just now when we were singing, not once," Max said.

"That's d-different. I—I—I . . . not in front of p-p-people," Lewis tried to explain.

"Look, buddy, I don't know anything about anything, but

I think you should give it a try. How else you ever gonna get rid of that stutter?"

Lewis didn't answer him. He sat for a long time, thinking. He sure would like to be in the play, especially with Max. But it was something he couldn't even allow himself to dream of. Getting up in front of a whole audience of people and talking! He couldn't manage to talk to the checkout lady at the supermarket without breaking into a sweat and stuttering. Yet, somehow, he knew Max was right. He'd never get better if he didn't try.

"Hey, why do you stutter, anyway?" Max asked him, breaking the silence.

Lewis shrugged. "I—I—I don't really kn-kn-know."

"I think you need more confidence, that's all," Max said.

More confidence, Lewis thought to himself. That's for sure.

"I think being in the play would help," Max said. "I want you to come with me tomorrow and at least check it out, okay?"

"Sh-sure," Lewis said, even though he knew there was no way.

"Look, it's getting pretty late. You want to camp out here with me tonight?" Max asked.

"Sh-sure. If it's okay."

"Hey, I just asked you, didn't I? It's okay with me if it's okay with your folks. I gotta warn you, though, it's a major battle against the mosquitoes. Like World War III, you dig?"

"I'll g-g-go ask m-my f-folks," Lewis said.

7

Normal People Use the Door

THE CLOUDS WERE THICK that night, and the woods were unusually quiet. There were no fireflies and even the mosquitoes seemed to have taken the night off, so the boys decided to sleep outside the small tent. The air was cool and there was more room.

Lewis was the first to feel the rain. A large drop landed right between his eyes, split in half, and ran down both sides of his nose like two tears.

"Psst. D-did you f-f-feel anything?" he asked Max, who was almost asleep. Before Max could answer, more drops hit them. Max sat up fast and slapped a mosquito on his neck.

"Oh, boy! Major hurricane, and the mosquitoes have zeroed in on us too. Red alert. Red alert! Everybody into the tent fast and batten down the hatches!"

It started to pour, and suddenly mosquitoes were everywhere. A big swarm filled the small tent. They were hungry for blood, especially Max's, dive-bombing every inch of his exposed skin. He was being eaten alive.

"Curse these foul creatures!" Max yelled as he flailed around inside of the tent, looking like a madman.

"We could g-g-go to my house," Lewis said as he watched Max slap himself in the face.

"Yeow!" A large bloodsucking mosquito came in for a landing on Max's leg and sank its needle deep into his flesh. "Aiii!" He howled in pain and smacked it hard. Unfortunately he also smacked one of the tent poles, hooking it with his arm and pulling it out. Half the tent crashed down on his head. Lewis burst out laughing.

"What are you laughing at?" Max said, pushing him in the chest. Lewis fell over backward, hitting the other pole, which broke right in half. Suddenly the two boys were trapped inside a dark, hot, collapsed tent. The mosquitoes kept eating away, and the rain hammered down in buckets.

"Abandon ship!" Max yelled. "Which way to the bomb shelter?" They scrambled to find their way out of the wet tent. Outside they were instantly soaked through to their skin. "It's, like, a natural disaster. Call in the Marines! The National Guard!" shouted Max. They threw all of their gear inside the tent, zipped it up, and, each grabbing an end, ran barefoot through the woods. When they reached the laurel hedge, lightning filled the sky, followed by thunder.

"Which door?" Max yelled as they crossed the backyard.

"Shh!" Lewis warned as he led him to the back porch. "Help me throw the tent up on the r-r-roof. C-come on. On th-three."

"What?" Max yelled. The thunder was so loud it was getting difficult to hear. "Let's use the door."

"They're all l-l-locked." Lewis lifted up his end of the tent. "One. T-t-two. Three." They threw the tent into the air as if it were a sack with a dead body in it. When it was almost up to the roof, it stopped. Caught by a sudden flash of lightning, it seemed suspended in midair like a photograph. A split second later it was dark again and the tent dropped, landing on top of the boys.

"Like wow. Like, we missed," Max said, peeking out from under the soggy lump of nylon.

Lewis was already working on another plan—to pull the tent up the drainpipe. He climbed up the pipe as far as he could, and Max handed him one end of the tent. The rain made everything slippery, and it was hard to see in the dark. The last bracket that held the pipe creaked as Lewis crawled up onto the roof. He prayed that it would hold Max as well.

Lewis leaned over the edge and instructed Max in the art of drainpipe climbing. Max was panting as he finally reached the top. Just as Lewis grabbed his hand, the last bracket gave way and the pipe split at its joints into separate sections, crumbling away under Max's feet.

Lewis pulled on Max's left hand with all his might as Max grabbed the roof's edge with his right hand. Max scraped a chunk of skin off his nose and tore his shirt, but he made it up.

"Wow. That was totally awesome. Like, I was face to face with Mr. Death himself. Man, I was staring right into his eyes. You saved my life, buddy."

Lewis laughed, turning his face up into the warm rain. "It's only t-twelve feet to the g-g-ground. I don't think you'd have d-died."

"Hey, you can't tell. Anyway, why didn't we use the door? Normal people use the door."

THE BOYS DRAGGED THE TENT through Lewis's bedroom and down the stairs, leaving a trail of water behind them. Max wanted to pitch the tent in the dining room, so they could camp out in rain-free comfort. While Lewis dried the nylon tent with his mother's hair dryer, Max dried himself off with a bath towel. He bandaged his nose and squeezed into a pair of Lewis's father's pajamas.

"Your parents are away for the whole night?" Max asked as they sorted out the gear. He tried to figure out how to set up the tent, since he couldn't very well sink the pegs into the dining-room floor.

Lewis thought hard. Should he tell Max the truth? "Eight w-w-weeks," he admitted.

"Eight weeks?" Max said. He suddenly noticed the mountain of pillows under the dining-room table and the pile of dirty dishes on the kitchen counter. "They left you alone here for eight weeks? All by yourself?" Max stared at Lewis. "Man, I've heard of liberal parents. I thought I had liberal parents. But yours, yours are totally awesome!"

"Y-y-you can't tell anyone. N-no one. It's a s-s-secret. I'm supposed to b-be at s-s-summer camp."

"Nobody knows?" Max sat down on the sofa to consider this amazing news. "You are kidding me? You mean, your parents don't know you're here? Where are they?"

"They're in the A-A-Arctic." Lewis wasn't sure this was such a good idea after all.

"The Arctic? As in the North Pole? Man, you are totally blowing my mind. I had you figured all wrong, you know that? I mean, you're even weirder than I am."

"You promise n-n-not to tell?"

"Hey, no sweat. Cross my heart and hope to die, and all that stuff," Max said. "But speaking of parents, I should call my dad. With this rainstorm he's probably having major cardiac arrest right now. Can I use the phone?"

Lewis hesitated.

"No problem. I'm one step ahead of you, my man. I'll tell him where I am. I'll just conveniently leave out the fact that your parents aren't here. The Arctic!" He laughed. "That kills me. It just kills me."

MAX AND LEWIS finally got the tent up by tying it with clothesline rope to the dining-room chandelier and to a wall light fixture. It was shaky, but there were no mosquitoes, which made Max very happy. "I think I've been bitten enough for one lifetime," he told Lewis as he passed him a can of beer. Max had discovered the six-pack in the pantry.

"I'm n-not sh-sure. My father w-w-won't—"

"Hey, trust me," Max said as he opened the can. "My dad always gives me beer. It's actually good for you. It's got vitamins and minerals. Hey, I wouldn't have even suggested it except that living alone and all, you should be very careful about nutrition."

Lewis wished that Max lived in North Renfield all year long. Boy, that would give old Stanley Flynn something to think about. If Lewis had Max around, Flynn would have to leave him alone. Max was as tall as Flynn and much bigger around. And Max was from New York City, which gave him a decided edge.

Lewis climbed into his sleeping bag and considered telling Max about Flynn and his gang. But what if Max thought he was a coward? It was hard to explain, anyway. Why did Flynn pick on him so much? He stuttered, no big deal. It didn't make much sense to Lewis. Oh, well. He'd tell Max some other time. It was fun camping out in the dining room, and Lewis wasn't going to spoil it by talking about Flynn.

"So, tomorrow you're gonna go over to the college with me and check out the play. Right?" asked Max.

"Sure," Lewis heard himself say. Well, why not? He could watch.

"Good," Max mumbled. His mumble turned into a little snore, and Max was asleep.

8

One of the Lost Boys

THE NEXT MORNING the boys made their way through the woods toward the college. Max whistled songs from *Peter Pan* and tapped out a rhythm on all the trees they passed. As they got closer to the campus, signs of "student life" were everywhere. Initials and messages were carved on the trees. "The Mooch loves Bambi Schwartz. Class of '84." "Who will have my baby? Gibbo. ZBT." Beer cans, liquor bottles, and cigarette butts were scattered around the ground, blending into the forest like bizarre species of flora.

At last they emerged into the morning sunlight, and Lewis squinted as his eyes adjusted to the brightness. A lawn dotted with dandelions spread uphill to a row of three-story dormitories. Beyond it were classrooms and administration buildings. The "old college," designed around a large central quadrangle of grass and big shady trees, had been built almost a century before. The dusty brick buildings were covered with ivy that curled around the white window frames and doorways. Surrounding these buildings was the "new campus," a recent addition of brick and concrete cubes. "Awesomely ugly," Max called it.

Summer school was in session, and students were lying around on the grass reading and talking. Others were playing Frisbee and touch football.

The theater building was a renovated church built of red brick and white clapboard. A wide brick staircase led up to three sets of heavy oak doors. Billowing cloth banners hung from flagpoles advertising the summer shows: *Peter Pan, The Importance of Being Earnest,* and *Sleuth.*

Lewis could hear a cacophony of noises as they walked up the stairs. When Max opened the door, he was overwhelmed by the activity inside. Up on the stage students were hammering and sawing and drilling; building walls, doorways, and furniture, palm trees and Indian tepees, and a huge pirate ship with tall masts and white sails. At the foot of the stage a bunch of kids Lewis's age stood around a piano singing along with an accompanist. Lewis recognized the song: "I Won't Grow Up." It was one he had sung with Max. He sang it quietly to himself as he followed Max down the center aisle.

On the auditorium floor several kids had rolled out wide pieces of white paper and were busy painting scenes: a starry night sky, a blue lagoon with mermaids and Indians in canoes. Back by the doors a young man in sweat clothes was teaching a row of girls and boys a dance step.

Lewis was fascinated by all the hammering and sawing and singing and dancing. All those kids his own age doing things he knew nothing about—it was wonderful and scary at the same time.

Max grabbed Lewis's arm and pulled him around to face a skinny man carrying a clipboard and wearing a whistle around his neck.

"Mr. Sweet, this is Lewis. He wants to be a Lost Boy," Max told him. "Lewis, meet Mr. Sweet, your new director."

"Can you sing?" Mr. Sweet asked Lewis.

"Like an angel," Max said, before Lewis could open his mouth.

"Perfect. We're desperate for Lost Boys. You're hired," Mr. Sweet said, patting Lewis on the back. "Max, take Larry here down—"

"Lewis," Max said.

"Of course. Take Lewis down to wardrobe to be measured for his costume, and then fill him in on what he's missed. Make sure Betsy gives him a parental-permission slip to fill out." Mr. Sweet looked down at his clipboard and made some notes. Max led Lewis away, toward the stage.

"That was easy," he said.

Lewis panicked. He'd only come to watch. He wasn't ready for this, not now, not ever. "I c-c-c-can't," he cried as he pulled away from Max and ran up the aisle toward the doors.

"Hey! What's going on?" Mr. Sweet yelled as Lewis rushed past him. Lewis reached the door and pushed hard. It wouldn't open. He pushed again, harder, and then he heard a thump from the other side. Then a loud curse. Lewis pushed again and this time the door swung open. There, on the top step, sat a high-school girl dressed in overalls. There were books and papers scattered all around her.

"Don't you know your right from your left?" She was mad. "How many times do we have to tell you kids? Come in on the left and go out the right. That was the left door."

Lewis just stood and stared, too embarrassed to move.

"Anyway, where are you going? You're supposed to be inside rehearsing. You can't just come and go as you please. You know the rules." She began picking up her papers and books. Lewis helped her, but he still couldn't talk, and he knew his face was bright red. He could feel it heating up.

"Well? Which one are you?" She stared at him. He stared

back. She sure was pretty, even though she was dressed like a boy, with high-top basketball sneakers, a sweatshirt, and greasy overalls. Her long brown hair was pulled back into a ponytail, and her hands were covered with grease.

"Hey, don't you talk, kid? Which one are you? Are you one of the Lost Boys? Or did they make you an animal? Huh?"

Lewis opened his mouth to answer her, but nothing came out. Not one word. So he did the next best thing. He ran down the steps, across the campus, and back into the woods.

Lewis sat high up in his favorite tree. He'd been there all day, thinking, wishing he'd never gone to the college theater. He thought over and over again about the girl he'd hit with the door. And about how mad she was. And about how mad he was that he couldn't speak.

The lights at the shopping center blinked on. It was getting late. Lewis was hungry. Something rustled in the bushes below him.

"I thought I'd find you here," Max yelled from the ground. "Don't make me come up there after you," he said in a television-cop voice. Then, in his own voice, "Because I doubt that I could."

Lewis looked down through the branches at Max. He was standing at the base of the tree with his hands on his hips. Lewis sighed. He wished he could jump from the tree and fly away, out over the woods like Peter Pan. But he couldn't, so he started down the tree. He would tell Max that there was no way he could handle the play. Max would be disappointed, and that bothered Lewis, but he just couldn't do it. No way.

He swung from the lowest branch and dropped to the ground next to Max.

"You remember that very pretty girl you flattened with a door at the theater today?"

Lewis nodded.

Max laughed. "That was Betsy, the assistant director. Cute, huh? We're extremely tight. I worked with her last summer. She wants to, uh, meet you again. Tomorrow."

Lewis shook his head. "I c-c-can't."

"You can, and you will," Max told him. "Listen, I've got to go home now, spend a little quality time with my dad. But I'll be by your pad tomorrow around ten. I'll rap three times on the back door."

Before Lewis could say anything, Max turned and disappeared into the woods.

9

Flynn Again

THE NEXT MORNING Max came by for Lewis, just as he had said he would. The two boys hiked through the woods toward the campus. Max seemed to be in an exceptionally—and, to Lewis, suspiciously—good mood.

"I have something to show you," Max told him with a grin. "A little action."

"A-action?" Lewis said.

"Yep. I decided that you need some diversion. And, buddy, did I find it." He smiled that smile again, making Lewis nervous.

When they reached the campus, instead of heading to the theater, Lewis followed Max as they crossed into a neighborhood of huge houses with perfectly manicured lawns. The rich people in town lived here.

Max turned to Lewis and winked. "It's time for Bikini Madness," he said. Max tiptoed down a private service driveway between two houses. The yards on both sides were hidden by high wooden fences, and Lewis could hear voices.

He stopped, but Max pulled him along, holding his finger to his lips.

There was a car parked in the drive and next to it a row of shiny new garbage cans. Max carefully climbed up on top of one of the cans and pointed to the can next to his. Lewis climbed up on it.

The two boys were just high enough to peek through the pointed fence slats. And, oh, boy, what they saw—girls, girls, girls! A dozen, at least, around a swimming pool. They were jumping and diving off the diving board, lying on lounge chairs and on towels, rubbing one another with suntan oil, reading magazines, and sipping cans of diet soda. Girls!

Lewis didn't recognize any of them, and he figured they were probably in high school. He looked at Max, who had that same mad grin on his face, only now it was wider and even crazier.

The back door of the house opened and another girl walked out into the yard. Lewis recognized this girl. Donna Bonita was in the eighth grade at his school, and she was best known for her highly developed figure, he told Max.

"I can see why," Max whispered back. "Va-va-voom!"

It was like being invisible, Lewis thought, and seeing into a secret world. Because of his stutter he had always been afraid to talk to the girls at school. Now he was only a few feet away, and they didn't even know he was there. Lucky thing too.

Suddenly there was a commotion inside the house, a lot of whistles and yelling, and the back door flew open. Out strutted Stanley Flynn, Wanker, and two of the weirder guys from Lewis's school—Head Mancewitz, who was named for his oversized head, and Butsy Fuller, who stank so bad that Mrs. Gallagher, a sixth-grade teacher, once threatened to give him a bath in front of the whole school if he didn't start washing up at home.

Lewis felt his knees go weak.

The girls jumped up, grabbing for their clothes and towels, and scattered like chickens when a fox shows up in the barnyard.

"Stanley Flynn! What do you think you're doing here?" one of the girls yelled. She stood her ground, hands defiantly on her hips. "You take your dumb friends and leave right this minute."

Flynn and his buddies just laughed.

"I mean it. I'll call my father," the girl threatened. "How did you get in here anyway?"

Just then Flynn happened to look in Lewis's direction. Lewis panicked. Flynn must have seen him! He instinctively stepped back and fell off the garbage can, making a tremendous racket.

Everyone in the backyard turned to look at the fence. Max jumped off his can and helped Lewis to his feet. They both ran down the alley as Stanley Flynn's ugly, sunburned face appeared at the top of the fence.

"Hey, hey, hey! Look who's spying on the girls! Come on, guys. Let's get them and teach them a lesson."

Max and Lewis doubled their speed, afraid to look back. But they heard the boys jump over the fence and run down the alley behind them. Lewis closed his eyes and ran so hard that his lungs started to ache and his body felt as if it might split in half.

"This way," Max panted, directing him down another service drive. The sound of footsteps and Flynn's voice still pursued them. It was a nightmare come true, and Lewis glanced over at Max half expecting him to change into some horrible monster and attack him.

But Max didn't. Instead he led Lewis through a maze of twists and turns, cutting through backyards and down streets until they made a full circle and ended up back in the first private drive. They slid underneath the car that was parked there and waited, their loud breathing barely drowning out their heartbeats.

Soon Flynn's feet went flying by, followed by three more pairs, and Lewis listened as their voices grew fainter and fainter. The two friends lay in the gravel until their pulses slowed down to normal.

"Well, I told you I was going to show you a little action," Max said finally. There was a long pause before he spoke again. "So, what do you think? Should we climb over the fence and say hi?"

WHEN THEY ARRIVED AT THE THEATER, still brushing gravel from their sweaty clothes, Betsy was waiting for them.

"Betsy, this is Lewis. Lewis, meet Betsy, the girl of my dreams."

"Hello, Lewis, nice to meet you—again," Betsy said with a grin, shaking his hand.

"I—I—I—I'm sorry," he said.

"He's sorry he hit you with the door. He stutters, but he doesn't stutter when he sings. I heard him. I want him to be in the play. A Lost Boy, with me. But he's afraid to try," Max said before Lewis could open his mouth.

"Well, that's a decision Lewis will have to make on his own," Betsy said. "But we sure could use you, Lewis. We need another Lost Boy. And we'll both help you along, won't we, Max?"

"You bet. So, what do you say, buddy? Are you in?" Max wanted to know.

But Lewis didn't answer, because he couldn't take his eyes off Betsy. She had the nicest smile he had ever seen.

"Lewis? Hey, wake up," Max said, shaking his arm.

"Okay. I—I'll t-try," he said.

"High five on that one, my man," Max said, slapping him on the back.

"I have a feeling you're going to enjoy it, Lewis." Betsy smiled as she handed him a script and a copy of the songs. "Okay, Max, take him to wardrobe, and I'll tell Norm—Mr. Sweet the good news. Oh, and Lewis, here's a parental-permission slip you need to have your parents fill out. And, remember, if you have any problems at all, you be sure and come to me."

"Okay. Th-thank you." Lewis watched her as she walked up onto the stage and disappeared into the wings. Yep. No doubt about it. He was definitely in love.

AFTER LEWIS HAD BEEN MEASURED for his costume, Max led him through the theater. The other kids were showing up and Mr. Sweet was frantically trying to organize everyone, yelling and blowing his whistle. He stopped to shake Lewis's hand.

"Glad to have you on board, Larry."

"L-L-L—"

"His name is Lewis!" Max yelled.

"Right. Of course. Lewis. Well, best you get started. I think you should just follow Max around for today. Learn the ropes, meet the other kids." Mr. Sweet blew his whistle again. "Everybody, I want you all to meet Lawrence. He's our new Lost Boy."

Max shook his head in disgust. But Lewis didn't mind. All of the kids came over and shook his hand and told him it was great to have him in the play. For the first time he felt as if he might have found a place where he could fit in. He didn't know any of these kids. Lots of them, he guessed, were from nearby towns. Maybe they'd be different.

It turned out that he had no time to be nervous that first

day. He was too busy following Max around and learning how to sing and dance. There were kids running around everywhere, and they were always bumping into each other or doing the wrong dance steps or forgetting the song lyrics. But everybody was having a good time.

"You're coming to dinner at my house tonight," Max told him between dance routines. "You'll get to meet my dad. And, more important, my dog, Rex."

Lewis could only nod as he counted out the dance steps in his head. One, two, three, four. Dinner at Max's sounded like a great idea, especially since his kitchen pantry was down to a box of crackers, one frozen pizza, and those packages of yeast. And Lewis didn't want to start picking through the neighbors' garbage cans any sooner than he had to.

10

A Perilous Trail of Cushions

AFTER REHEARSAL the two boys went back to Lewis's house and sneaked his bicycle out of the basement window. Max sat between the handlebars and Lewis pedaled, groaning all the way, to Max's house, where Max's father had dinner ready for them.

"Dig in, boys," Mr. Winkler said as he put the plates down in front of Lewis and Max.

"Thanks, Phil," Max said.

Mr. Winkler insisted on being called by his first name. Even by his own son. It sounded pretty weird to Lewis, and so he avoided the whole issue by never talking to Max's father first.

Lewis stared down at his plate, at the unrecognizable food, then sneaked a quick look at Max, who was grimacing.

"Looks like a burnt, skinny pancake with whipped cream to me," Max whispered, as Phil sat down at the table. "Ah, Phil, could I have a moment of your time, please? What's this junk inside of my pancake?"

"That 'junk' inside happens to be caviar, you boorish oaf of a son of mine," Phil said. "And as for your 'pancake,' it's a buckwheat crêpe topped with crème fraîche. Haven't you learned anything about fine food in five years in New York City, or is your mother, bless her heart, still stuffing you with peanut-butter-and-Marshmallow Fluff sandwiches?"

"Yecch," was all Max could say. He turned to Lewis and shrugged as they both took their first tentative bites.

The next course was just as strange, with some kind of squiggly-shaped cold noodles mixed with vegetables that Lewis had never seen before. Both boys ate dutifully, exchanging rueful glances. Whenever Phil wasn't watching, they fed Rex the Wonder Dog helpings from their plates. Rex the Wonder Dog, Max's black Labrador, seemed pleased with this, and he strategically placed himself under the table between the two boys.

Lewis didn't know what to make of Phil. He wasn't at all like most fathers he'd met. He seemed happier, always joking around and telling stories. According to Max he spent all of his free time either in the oversized kitchen or outside in his vegetable and herb garden. Phil was a psychology professor at the college but was most famous for his evening cooking classes, which he taught right in his own house.

Lewis's father usually stayed out of the kitchen when he was home, except for Sunday mornings, when he turned out his "famous" scrambled eggs with cheese and peppers. Lewis's mother thought that he made much more of a mess in the kitchen than was necessary, and she was always the one left to clean it up. Yet here was Max's father, in a long white apron, dashing around a kitchen crowded with pots and pans hanging from the ceiling, fancy appliances, cookbooks, and the biggest stove and refrigerator Lewis had ever seen. Phil even hummed when he cooked. And sang. He sure wasn't a normal father. Fun, but not normal.

"HE THINKS HE'S THE GALLOPING GOURMET," Max said as they pedaled their bikes away from the house. "That means I never get anything regular to eat. He experiments on me. And now on you too." Max laughed, swerving down the middle of the deserted road.

They didn't have much time. Phil had given Max permission to sleep over at Lewis's, but he'd insisted that Max call immediately after getting there. At first he'd wanted to drive them to Lewis's. "Kids on bikes at night are not safe," he'd said.

"Come on. Guys do it all the time," Max had said. "It's all under control, Phil." Max slapped his father on the back. "We'll be at Lewis's before you can say 'quiche lorraine.' "

The truth, however, was that they made one slight detour, to the Skippy Dog stand on Route 22. There they each ordered two Superdog Specials, with all the trimmings.

"I'm always starving after Phil's din-dins," Max admitted. "But Rex sure eats well. I guess he's a gourmet too." He laughed, paid for the hot dogs with a twenty-dollar bill, and stuffed the change into Lewis's back pocket.

"Hey, w-w-what are you doing?" he protested.

"No sweat. I took it from Phil's wallet."

Lewis stared at his friend.

"Really. Hey, it's cool. It's a game we play. I don't go overboard and he pretends not to notice. He feels real bad about the divorce. So I get 'money instead of Mom' for the summer. Sort of." Max tried to explain, but Lewis didn't really understand. He would never take money from his father's wallet without asking first. Phil and Max sure had a strange relationship.

"Look, you need money to eat, don't you?" Max reasoned.

Lewis nodded. He sure did.

"Then keep the bucks. It's all right." Max jammed the last of his hot dog into his mouth and washed it down with his soda.

Lewis kept the money.

THE BOYS HID THEIR BIKES IN THE WOODS, waited until the coast was clear, and then sprinted across the darkened lawn. Lewis slid under the porch and Max followed.

"Isn't there any other way in?" Max asked. "I can't fit under here."

"No," Lewis said. "It's n-not s-s-safe to use the d-doors."

"We put that drainpipe permanently out of commission, huh?" Max asked.

"Yep." Lewis crawled ahead and dropped through the window into the basement. He turned on the flashlight he'd left there on his way out.

"I've got to fit through this little window?" Max gasped, poking his head through. "And drop all that way? You've got to be kidding."

"Y-y-you can do it," Lewis told him.

"Sure, easy for you to say." Max lowered himself in and dropped, raising a cloud of dust. "We've got to start using the doors, man, if I'm gonna be spending a lot of time here. I can't risk my life every day."

As the boys made their way upstairs, Lewis recited the house rules to Max: One, no opening any curtains, two, no loud music or television, and three, try not to break anything.

"Don't w-worry about the l-lights," he said. "Those y-y-you can turn on and off w-whenever. The neigh-neigh-neighbors think it's the l-light ti-timer."

Max turned on the light, looked around, and whistled.

"Awesome. Totally," he said. "I didn't know you had it in you, kid."

The tent was still pitched in the dining room, and Lewis's original pillow-and-blanket camp was intact under the table. Clothes were hanging from chairs, stairs, and light fixtures. Dirty dishes and pots and pans covered the table and all the counters in the kitchen.

Max officially named the house "The Lost Boys' Hideaway" and suggested that a new adventure was in order. And he had just the idea: The two boys removed all the books from the bookshelves and laid them out all through the upstairs, like stepping stones crossing a stream filled with deadly piranha.

The idea was to travel through the house without ever touching the floor once.

In Lewis's bedroom the carpeted floor became a crocodile-filled lagoon. From his bed the boys had to jump to the closet door, land with their feet on the doorknob, and swing around to the dresser. Hanging from the bookshelf, they moved, hand over hand, above the boiling lava pit—better known as the radiator—and dropped to Lewis's desk. Finally a big leap to the upside-down wastebasket and a short hop to the first book in Piranha River.

The books, or stones, led them down the river—the hallway—to the harrowing white rapids—the staircase. A quick slide down the banister followed by a flip and a swing of the legs landed them in the Secret Fortress—the living room.

Then they traveled along a perilous trail of cushions borrowed from the chairs and sofas, to the dining room. A wide and dangerous chasm lay between the last dining-room chair and an elaborate arrangement of pots and pans in the kitchen. With good balance and a lot of luck that chasm could be crossed. Lewis managed it eight out of ten tries. Max went crashing to the floor much more often. But he swore to Lewis that he'd be ten out of ten by the end of the summer or he'd chop his right foot off and feed it to a crocodile.

After a particularly painful tumble Max looked up from the floor and said, "Let's rehearse our songs for a while, okay?"

Lewis smiled. "Sh-sure."

Sheet music in hand, the boys sang together, learning the lyrics to the songs in *Peter Pan.*

By unlucky coincidence, at that moment Frances Rupert happened to be out walking Bunny, and she could hear . . . What was it she heard? . . . voices, young boys' voices, singing a strangely familiar song. Only, she couldn't quite place the song, nor could she tell where the voices were coming from. So she decided to investigate, starting in the middle of the street, walking in ever-widening circles. Bunny followed close behind, her funny ears flipped back, her nose up in the air sniffing. She heard the voices too.

Lewis and Max were hopping merrily from book to book and singing a song of pirates and Indians, unaware of the real danger approaching. The boys fell silent as Max prepared to jump the chasm one last time, and that's when they heard Bunny yapping. What luck! Two more notes, and Mrs. Rupert would have discovered Lewis's secret life for sure. The boys held their breath. Mrs. Rupert stood for some time looking from the woods to the house. Finally she motioned for Bunny to follow, and she headed down the driveway to the street.

Whew! A close call. Lewis and Max immediately proclaimed Rule Number Four: No singing out loud, except in the basement.

THE NEXT MORNING, Lewis awoke to the sound of the dishwasher. He walked into the kitchen to see Max standing by the sink drinking a glass of water. The counters and the table were all cleared off.

"Morning. I woke up early, so I thought I'd wash some of the dishes for you. Don't worry, I know how to run that beast. Just load it up and throw in three big scoops of that detergent over there," Max said, pointing to the box on the pantry shelf.

Detergent? Lewis took a closer look. "This is m-m-m-milk."

"Really?" Max walked over and picked up the box. "Well, I'll be. Powdered milk. Well, hey, it's a mistake anybody could make, right? I mean, it looks like detergent." He shut off the dishwasher. "Tell you what, let's not open it. What do you say? It could be real messy."

Lewis unlatched the door and opened it. Max was right. Everything was covered with hot milk.

"I told you not to open it," Max said, taking a drink of water.

"At l-least you didn't try to do my l-l-laundry," Lewis said.

Max spit water out all over the floor and ran for the basement stairs. Lewis was right behind him.

Opening up the washer, Lewis pulled out his soggy jeans. Gobs of sticky white goo were packed into all the pockets. The washing machine was like a big bowl of clothes cereal.

"Hey, I figured, what difference would it make?" Max shrugged. "I couldn't find any laundry detergent, so I used the dishwashing detergent. Soap's soap, right?"

"Unless it's m-m-milk," Lewis said. And both boys burst out laughing. Then they closed the washer lid and went back upstairs. Maybe if they ignored the mess, it would go away.

Lewis had another problem to take care of. He needed a signed permission slip from his parents. He and Max went into the library, and Lewis practiced his father's signature.

He copied it from a letter in the desk, just as he'd done when he wrote the letter to the camp director.

"Hey, let me handle that," Max said. "I'm a master of forgery. Look at this." He took a fake ID card from his wallet and showed it to Lewis. It had Max's photo, and it listed his age as twenty-one, which was the legal drinking age in New York.

"V-v-very impressive," Lewis said.

"It's great for picking up college chicks," Max said with a wink. Lewis laughed at the thought of Max trying to pick up women in some New York bar.

"Here we go. How's that look?" Max asked as he finished the signature at the bottom of the form letter. Lewis examined it carefully.

"It looks j-j-just like m-m-my father's."

"It's a talent you have to be born with," Max said.

"Thanks," Lewis said, and he folded up the letter and put it in his pocket. It was time to go to rehearsal. Lewis felt more confident today. And his stutter seemed a little bit better already.

11

Remember Superman

LEWIS GREW MORE AND MORE CONFIDENT. Strange as it seemed, he never stuttered when he sang. Because he only had two lines to speak in the entire play, they weren't much of a problem. Could it be that his stutter was actually disappearing?

Mr. Sweet, however, was losing his voice from shouting. How could anybody yell so much? Lewis wondered. Even when he wasn't mad, he still liked to yell, especially at Betsy Harris. Betsy was not only the assistant director, but she was also playing the role of Wendy Darling, the girl Peter Pan takes back to Never-Never Land so she can be a mother to all the Lost Boys. Mr. Sweet yelled at her about almost everything. Do this! Do that! Get those kids in order! Why don't those children know their lines?

Lewis had a full-blown crush on Betsy ever since the day he had knocked her over with the door. He hated it when Mr. Sweet yelled at her. He even got up the nerve to tell Betsy about it one afternoon. But she only smiled at him and said, "Mr. Sweet's just nervous. That's all. He's doesn't mean anything bad by it."

Backstage someone said that Mr. Sweet and Betsy were in love. No way, thought Lewis. Betsy was still in high school and Mr. Sweet had already graduated from college. He'd ask Max just to be sure. Max and Betsy had been friends ever since Max had joined the summer productions. Max would know.

Betsy was a senior at Greenridge High, which was about ten miles away. She worked at a gas station part time and rode a motorcycle to rehearsals. Each morning Lewis sat on the theater steps and waited for her to arrive, so he could watch her when she took off her motorcycle helmet. Most days she wore jeans and a sweatshirt that had a Harley-Davidson logo on the back. Lewis, his fingers tapping out a tune on his knees, would watch Betsy's long legs pull her up the steep hill from the parking lot. He'd smile at her when she got close enough, and she'd smile back.

"Good morning, Mr. Mysterious. Are you all ready to work?" she always said. Betsy called Lewis "Mr. Mysterious" because he hardly talked during rehearsals. What Betsy didn't know was he'd talked more in the last three weeks than he had all year in school.

It was during one of these daily rituals that Betsy, instead of heading right into the theater, sat down with Lewis on the steps. Lewis's heart jumped. Maybe she was going to ask him for something—something like a date! His fingers tapped a faster tune on his knees as he waited for her to speak. Then he had an awful thought. Maybe she was going to kick him out of the show. But why would she do that? He was doing so well. He had learned all the dance steps, which mostly consisted of running, jumping, and doing somersaults and cartwheels. All he had to do was end up in the right spot at the right time and not bump into anybody. Other than a couple of stutters during the last week, his performance was terrific. Even Mr. Sweet said so. So what did Betsy want? Whatever it was, she was taking her good old time about it.

"Lewis, Arnie Lesser has to have his appendix taken out," she finally said.

"Yeah? Th-that's too bad," Lewis said. Arnie was playing the role of John Darling, the older of Wendy's brothers. He goes off to Never-Never Land with Peter Pan too. It was a very big role.

"He's going to leave the show. We're going to have to replace him," she said.

"Oh. W-with who?" Lewis asked. He wondered if Max was going to get the part. That sure would be great.

Betsy turned and smiled at him. "Mr. Sweet and I are both hoping you'll agree to do it."

Lewis was dumbstruck. He couldn't think of anything to say. Luckily Betsy kept right on talking.

"You look the part. You're exactly the right size. And your singing voice is beautiful. You'd be perfect. Mr. Sweet thinks so too." Betsy gave him a long, slow look—a specialty of hers. "I'll help you with the lines if you're worried about your stutter. You'll be the best. I just know it."

Lewis looked up at Betsy, wishing he could say yes. But he couldn't. John Darling? That would mean having to speak lots of lines, hundreds of words. And he'd have to sing parts of songs all by himself. In front of all those people.

Playing John Darling would be asking for trouble. And trouble came up often enough in real life on its own. Lewis looked away from Betsy and stared down at a trail of ants marching across the steps.

"Think about it, okay?" Betsy said. "But let me know soon." She got up and went into the theater, leaving Lewis and the ants alone on the steps.

WHEN MAX HEARD that Betsy had offered Lewis the role of John Darling, it was all he could talk about. "It's a lead," he kept telling Lewis, making him even more nervous. "This could be your big break. No telling what could happen next! Broadway. The silver screen. A three-picture deal with Warner Brothers. Your own television series with Cybill Shepherd."

Lewis tried to explain that his stutter made it almost impossible for him to do a speaking role in front of so many people, but Max didn't care about the risks.

"Lewis, you've got to try," he said. "I'd do it if they asked me. And you know how much I hate heights."

Lewis wasn't Max, not by a long way. Yet he did decide to do it in the end. Not because he woke up one morning without a stuttering problem. But because of the "three good reasons" that Max kept reciting to him over and over again. One, he would never change if he didn't try. Two, he'd get to work more with the "ever beautiful" Betsy. And three, Max wasn't going to let him say no.

"OKAY. NOW, JUST RELAX," Mr. Sweet told Lewis as Betsy and a stagehand attached a wire to the back of the tight leather harness strapped around his body. It was two days later, and already they were working hard with Lewis. Today was "flying" day.

"We're just going to lift you up and down a few times, to get you used to it," Mr. Sweet said. He gave the thumbs-up sign to the stagehands in the wings who were holding the ropes. Lewis felt a tug at his back, and his feet left the ground. He fell forward, throwing his hands in front of him to cushion his fall. Only, he didn't fall. He went up.

He went up and down as Mr. Sweet yelled out instructions to the stagehands, and each time Lewis left the ground he liked it more. As John Darling he would be singing and flying in the biggest number in the show, "I'm Flying," at the end of the first act. He'd have to soar back and forth across the stage with four other actors. It was very tricky business that took lots of stagehands in the wings and a lot of practice.

"We're going to take you up a little higher now," Mr. Sweet yelled. "Arch your back. Put your arms out as if you're swimming. Point in the direction you want to go."

Lewis rose almost to the top of the proscenium arch over the stage. He could see all the ropes and pulleys and lights hanging from the rafters as he sailed back and forth. Everyone in the theater stopped what they were doing to watch. Even the janitor stopped sweeping. Below him Betsy was waving and smiling, and all the girls and boys cheered as he zoomed across the stage. He felt as if he were really flying.

"Lift your head, arch your back more. Bend!" Mr. Sweet kept barking out orders. "Remember Superman. Remember Icarus."

"Who?" Lewis shouted back as he started to spin in circles.

"Remember Mary Poppins," Betsy yelled.

"Remember the fairies, you f-f-f-fairy," someone else shouted from the back of the theater. Everyone turned. There in the open doorway stood Stanley Flynn.

"Only fairies fly," he yelled, and he and his gang came charging into the theater, letting out war whoops.

Lewis hung helplessly in the air, watching as Flynn and his usual partners-in-crime, Butsy Fuller, Cueball, Cycle, Wanker, and Cheese, attacked, taking everyone by surprise. They ran through the theater, overturning tables and chairs, scattering scripts in the air, and kicking holes in the scenery.

"Down with fairies," Flynn shrieked, and the rest of the

gang chanted, "Down with fairies! Down with fairies! Down with fairies!"

They jumped up onto the stage, and Cueball leapt into the air, trying to reach Lewis, who was frozen in space. Lewis couldn't move at all, except to spin around and around slowly above the confusion, like an astronaut floating above the earth.

"Get him! Get him!" the hoodlums yelled as they jumped at Lewis's feet. He tucked his legs up to his chest and turned himself into a ball. The cast and crew stood stunned. Betsy ran up behind Flynn and gave him a solid kick in the rear.

"Get out of here, you dumb kids, before I break your necks!"

Flynn whirled around, and Lewis could see that he couldn't believe a girl had had the nerve to kick him.

Then the crew rallied behind Betsy, and the pirates and Indians and the Lost Boys of Never-Never Land surrounded Flynn and his gang. Just as Flynn swung a punch at one of the stagehands, someone rang the fire alarm. It started clanging, and in less than a minute the campus police ran in. Flynn and his gang scattered in all directions. Lewis was still curled in a ball, hanging above the chaos, miserably aware that this was all his fault.

Mr. Sweet and Betsy were trying to restore order when a crew member finally lowered Lewis to the floor. Unclipped from his wire, he ran, harness and all, through the dark backstage area and out the emergency fire door into the bright afternoon. He pulled his bike out of the bike rack and pedaled away.

12

A Very Bad Day

LEWIS SAT ALONE under a big umbrella at one of the wooden picnic tables outside of Skippy Dog. Happy hot dogs with little hands and feet and little white chef's hats on their hot-dog heads were painted on the umbrella above his head. Dancing around them were smiling bottles of mustard and ketchup. They all looked very pleased with life, unlike Lewis, who did not feel the least bit pleased about anything. He sat halfheartedly chewing his Superdog Special with fried onions, relish, ketchup, and mustard. His Superdog didn't have hands or feet, and the mustard and ketchup bottles on his table didn't dance. They didn't move at all, unless Lewis picked them up and squeezed them. His Superdog Special tasted just awful. *Probably because I'm so unhappy,* he thought.

The hot-dog stand was almost deserted, since it was too late for lunch and too early for supper, and the parking lot was empty when Betsy zipped in on her motorcycle.

Lewis looked up. He wanted to ignore her, but he

couldn't resist watching Betsy take her helmet off. And at that moment life did seem brighter. But he was determined to remain miserable, so he looked back down at the tabletop, pretending to study the engravings in the wood.

Betsy was sure to ask him about Flynn. How was he going to explain it? He knew very well what would happen then. Everyone would want to know why he didn't stand up for himself. And soon they'd begin to notice his stutter, and then the teasing would begin. Just like before. Just like always. He was responsible for everything that had happened. If he hadn't been in the play, Flynn and his cronies would never have bothered terrorizing the theater.

"Can I have a bite?" Betsy asked as she sat down across from him. Max must have told her he'd be here, Lewis figured, as he nudged his Superdog across the table.

"Whew! Woof! This smells awful! Are you actually eating this thing?" she asked, passing the hot dog back to him. "I wasn't really hungry, anyway."

Lewis obstinately took a big bite of the Superdog, stuffing as much of it into his mouth as he could fit. He couldn't very well talk with his mouth full.

They just sat there. Betsy, with her head in her hands, watched Lewis. And Lewis devoured his hot dog and watched Betsy. It was a stand-off.

Betsy finally broke the silence. "You don't have to tell me anything if you don't want to. But if I can help, just let me know, okay?" She got up. "See you at rehearsal tomorrow, John Darling."

She waved from her motorcycle, and then she roared off down Route 22.

LEWIS PEDALED FAST on Linden Street's slight grade, down to the intersection of Sawmill Lane. On the corner he cut through the fire-station parking lot to get a head start on the big hill.

He was usually extra careful here, this close to home. Someone might recognize him. But today he was so upset that nothing else mattered. He pedaled right up the middle of the street and thought about Flynn. "I'd like to b-b-bash that Flynn's face in," he said aloud. "I hate Stanley Flynn. I hate Stanley Flynn!" he yelled at the top of his lungs.

He flew over the top of Sawmill Hill and started down the other side, gaining speed. The wind in his face felt good. He was really cooking now, imagining Flynn and his gang at the bottom, lined up in a row. One by one he rammed them with his bike. And one by one they fell like bowling pins.

Lewis was going too fast when the entrance to the dirt path came up, and he knew it. But he didn't care. At that moment he didn't care about anything or anybody, including himself. When he hit a big rock in the middle of the path, his bike stopped dead. His hands were torn from the handlebars and he catapulted forward as the bike slid out from underneath him and slammed into the trees.

Lewis sat up slowly. He had cuts on the palms of his hands and on his elbows. His pants were torn at both knees. But nothing hurt too badly. He stood up and checked the bike. The front tire was flat and the rim was bent out of shape, but everything else seemed intact. If Flynn hadn't ruined everything at rehearsal, this wouldn't have happened, he thought. Lewis was so mad that his head started to ache. He wanted to hurt Flynn, but Flynn wasn't there. Instead he punched a tree so hard that his knuckles started to bleed. He picked up his bike and began to push it home. It looked as if it might rain. Swell. Why not? Everything else was going wrong.

All the way home he thought about Stanley Flynn. What would become of Flynn when he grew up? Probably he was headed for prison. Death row, Lewis thought with satisfaction. As for the rest of the gang, well, they'd probably all end up in adjoining cells with their leader.

He was so busy imagining Flynn behind bars that he forgot to see if the coast was clear before he came out of the woods into his yard. In full view of the street and the Ruperts' house, Lewis leaned the bike up against the porch and headed for the front door. Reality hit him just as he reached the top step, and he turned and ran back down the steps, grabbed his bike, and dived under the porch. Metal and wood and body crashed together onto the dirt.

It was too late.

Like a storm trooper Mrs. Rupert marched up the driveway. Bunny raced ahead of her and reached Lewis first, nipping at his shirt sleeve and licking his face.

"Go home!" Lewis ordered in a heavy whisper. But Bunny continued dancing about, yapping and raising dust. Before Lewis could quiet her, he heard that all-too-familiar voice.

"Lewis? Lewis Dee? Is that you under there? What are you doing under the porch, dear? Is something wrong? Where are your mother and father?"

Lewis was lying face down in the cool dirt. He took a long, deep breath and turned his head, hoping that somehow he wouldn't see what he knew was out there waiting for him. But he recognized the lime-green housecoat and those spindly legs. It was definitely Frances Rupert.

He slid out from under the porch and brushed the dirt off his clothes. There was no use pretending. Little beads of sweat formed on his forehead, and he felt his throat tightening up. In just one afternoon everything he'd worked so hard for was gone. And it was Stanley Flynn's fault. All of it. The bike. His bloody lip. The play. Mrs. Rupert. Bunny. And every other bad thing that had happened to him on this stupid day.

Mrs. Rupert rattled on. ". . . And your parents? Where are they? Didn't they go to the North Pole, or wherever it was they were going? Who can keep track with that father of yours, always off to one crazy place or another. Your poor mother, I don't know how she . . . I'm sorry, dear. Am I going too fast for you? I always forget to slow down for you. You just take your time and I'll try to help you," she said, without slowing down at all.

Lewis didn't like to lie and he wasn't very good at it, because of his stutter. But telling the truth was out of the question.

"You don't look at all well, Lewis. Are you feeling all right? You're not sick, are you? Who's taking care of you?"

"I—I—I—I'm f-f-fine," he said. This was really going to be hard.

"Oh, dear. Oh, my. What happened to your lip? And your hands? Are those nasty boys picking on you again?" Mrs. Rupert always asked at least two questions at the same time. Lewis never knew which question to answer first, and it made him stutter even worse. If it weren't for the fact that Mrs. Rupert answered most of her own questions anyway, he wouldn't be able to talk to her at all. This time he touched his lip with his finger and nodded his head.

"You poor, poor boy. Those bullies should be locked up. I have half a mind to call the police. Where are your parents? You're not here all alone, are you? Of course you're not. But why aren't you at camp? Has it ended already?"

That was at least four questions, maybe five. This was not going well. He'd better start making something up quick.

"C-c-camp is o-o-over." As soon as he said it, he realized it was a mistake. He could see from the expression on Mrs. Rupert's face that more questions were on the way.

"Camp is over? Oh, goodness. And I thought you were going for the whole summer. Did you enjoy camp? Your mother told me all about it. It sounds like a wonderful, wonderful place. You must have just gotten home or I would have noticed. When did you come home? Yesterday? Who's staying here with you? Certainly you're not here all alone."

Lewis's head was spinning. He mentally reviewed all of her questions, then he took a stab at one of the last ones.

"I'm staying with my f-f-f-f . . ."

"Your father's . . . your father's what?" Mrs. Rupert was getting excited, as if she were on a game show trying to win a new car or a dishwasher.

"M-m-m-m . . ." Lewis couldn't seem to get "my friend" out.

"Your father's mother? Your grandmother!" She was jumping up and down now, sure she had gotten one of the answers right. Definitely worth a free trip to Hawaii.

Grandmother seemed like a safe answer, so Lewis nodded.

"Is she staying with you now? Here?"

He kept right on nodding. What the heck. It was perfect. If Mrs. Rupert thought that his grandmother was staying with him, she wouldn't make a fuss. He wouldn't have to sneak around anymore. Of course, this would make things really complicated when his parents came home, but that was going to be a disaster no matter how things turned out.

Lewis's relief was short-lived, however. Mrs. Rupert wanted to meet his grandmother.

"To welcome her to the neighborhood. And to see if there's anything at all I can do to help. Anything at all" was how she put it.

It took another ten minutes of *Twenty Questions* and stuttering before Lewis could convince her not to come inside the house with him. But there was a trade-off. Mrs. Rupert made him promise to have his grandmother call her by the next day.

"I mean, what she must think of me? She must think I'm a terrible neighbor. I'll never forgive your mother for not telling me that she was coming to stay. The poor dear must be dying for some company."

Lewis crawled back under the porch after Mrs. Rupert was out of sight. He lay there awhile, spinning the back tire of his bike and listening to the clicking of the gears. The setting sun passed through the cracks in the porch floor and lit up the dust around him, making swirling shafts of orange light. *I'm having a bad day,* he thought to himself. *A very bad day.*

13

The Early-Morning Hell's Angel

IT WAS LATE THAT NIGHT and Lewis felt awful. It wasn't because of Stanley Flynn, or his broken bike, or even being caught by Mrs. Rupert. He felt physically awful. Sick, in fact. He sat on the bathroom floor and hugged the bathtub, hoping that he wouldn't have to throw up again. The cool porcelain tub felt good against his hot and sweaty cheek. There was nothing left in his stomach to get rid of, but his brain continued to send the vomit order south. And as if that weren't bad enough, he had diarrhea. His stomach was hard as a rock, which scared him because it had never felt that way before. He gripped the tub tightly, trying to stop his dizziness.

When Lewis had felt the first twinge in his stomach, he thought it was just because of his miserable day. That kind of day was enough to make anyone sick. And Lewis was really sick. Sick as a dog. Dog? Dog. Hot dog. Oh, boy. Lewis thought of his dinner, and he had a vision of leering Superdogs prancing around the bathroom, tap-dancing on the rim of the bathtub. They were pointing and laughing and whispering to the ketchup and mustard bottles with them, and their little feet were making a racket, tap-tap-tapping away.

This was serious, Lewis realized. He'd been sick before, but nothing like this. He felt as if he wanted to die. If only his mother were there, she'd know what to do. She'd know whether or not to call a doctor. Lewis couldn't call a doctor. If a doctor ever came into the house, he'd take one look and Lewis's summer secret would blow sky-high. He couldn't call Max, either, because his father would be sure to answer the phone. Oh, boy, just thinking about Max's father made him picture all those awful things Phil concocted for dinner. . . . Whoops! He barely made it to the toilet that time, and the dancing hot dogs were really laughing at him now. Then they were joined by Rex the Wonder Dog, who was sitting in the bathtub barking. He was wearing shiny black shoes on his paws and he was tap-dancing. Suddenly the bathroom was crowded. Max and Phil and Stanley Flynn and Cycle and Cheese were all pointing and laughing. Lewis's head was spinning and he felt hot. Now Betsy was singing and dancing on the sink. Betsy? He could call Betsy.

Lewis crawled out of the bathroom, leaving the noisy party behind him. He was so weak and dizzy, he could barely stand up. But he made it to the telephone, and he dialed Betsy's number. One. Two. Three rings. He looked at the clock and focused his bleary eyes on the illuminated digits. Four A.M. A very groggy man answered. Uh-oh. Betsy's father. Lewis almost hung up, but he knew he had no choice now.

"Could I—I—I p-please s-s-speak to B-B-Betsy, please?" he asked. The man didn't say anything. There was a very long pause, and then Lewis heard Betsy's sleepy voice. He couldn't help it. He started to cry.

FRANCES RUPERT never slept very well, and she liked to wander around her house in the middle of the night. She just happened to be down in the kitchen that night, talking to Bunny, when she heard a motorcycle roaring down the street. The single headlight arched across her kitchen ceiling as the bike passed the house and pulled into the Dees' driveway. From the window Mrs. Rupert watched a mysterious figure dismount and head for the front door. She was just about to pick up the phone and call the police when she saw the door open. And to her surprise there was Lewis, letting the stranger into his house. Well! Frances Rupert was flabbergasted. Who was this early-morning Hell's Angel? And why was he visiting Lewis and his grandmother at such an ungodly hour? Mrs. Rupert was certainly not going back to bed now.

"ARE YOU ALONE?" Lewis asked as he opened the front door a crack.

"Completely," Betsy assured him. "Come on. Open up." Lewis's phone call had scared her. He wouldn't explain anything on the phone, only that he was alone, really sick, and that he needed her.

Lewis opened the door, and Betsy walked into the living room. She stopped dead, and for a moment she couldn't speak. She even forgot about Lewis, who was holding himself up by the doorknob. Betsy had stepped through the front door of a very ordinary-looking house, and now she was faced with madness.

The living room looked like a jungle, with all the furniture turned upside down. Ropes and string were tied to everything, crisscrossing the room, turning it into a giant, fantastic maze. Betsy had to walk under, around, and through it to get to the dining room, where there was a tent pitched next to the dining-room table. Under the table there seemed to be a little house, with piles of pillows and blankets. There was even a portable television set and a lamp.

"What's going on here, Lewis?" she asked. She turned back to find him lying on the floor, looking very white, very sick, and not too concerned with the peculiar interior design of the house.

"Lewis! Oh, Lewis." Betsy knelt and hugged him. Lewis closed his eyes and thought that it felt good and that maybe he wasn't going to die after all.

"I TOLD YOU that hot dog smelled terrible," Betsy reminded him as she wiped his face with cool washcloth. "I'm going to call the Board of Health on that place."

Lewis looked up at her. "Thanks f-for c-c-coming over."

"Sure. Now stay quiet. Tomorrow you can—and will—explain everything to me." She tucked his sheet and blanket in tight and kissed him on the forehead. Sick or not sick, he was in love.

Lewis had refused to go to the hospital. He got so upset that Betsy thought it would be better to keep him at home. She called her own family doctor, waking her, of course, and described Lewis's symptoms over the phone. It was mild food poisoning. As long as Betsy stayed with him and it didn't seem to get any worse, the doctor thought that Lewis would be all right at home. The worst of it seemed to be over. Betsy was to keep him quiet and make sure he drank lots of water.

When morning came, Betsy sat on the floor under the dining-room table next to Lewis, who was curled up on his mattress of pillows. She wiped his forehead and listened as Lewis told her the true story of his summer. He told her everything. She sat and listened and didn't say a word. When he finally drifted off to sleep, Betsy crawled into the nearby tent, exhausted, and fell asleep in minutes.

BREAKFAST WAS QUIET. Lewis wasn't talking because he barely had the strength to sit up. He didn't feel sick anymore, but he felt as if somebody had stuck a needle into him and drained out all his blood, then had thrown him off the roof a dozen times, and then had driven a car over him.

Lewis watched Betsy as she made him toast. He figured she wasn't talking because she was too busy thinking. She had that worried, concentrating look on her face. He was sure that she was thinking about what to do about him. After last night's episode something would have to change. But at least now he might not have to stay with the Ruperts. If he worked it out right, maybe he could get Betsy to come and stay with him. Living alone had its pitfalls, Lewis realized. No one was there to worry about you. You could fall or get sick and no one would know. He wondered how adults got used to not having parents around to worry.

"You know, this is really a difficult situation," Betsy finally said, as they sat across from each other at the table.

Lewis nodded.

"I mean, I feel responsible for you now."

He waited.

"Look at what happened last night. What if nobody had been home when you called?"

Lewis shrugged his shoulders and put on his meekest face.

Betsy looked out the window into the yard. Lewis felt guilty as he watched her. Now was the time for him to speak up.

"I kn-kn-know you c-c-can't st-stay h-here. . . ." He

paused to see if she'd jump in and say, yes, she could. She didn't. "B-b-b-but maybe Max c-could."

"Max is not exactly what I'd call a responsible adult," Betsy pointed out. "He's barely a responsible kid."

Still, she could see that the idea had possibilities. The kitchen filled up with "What ifs" and "How abouts" and "Maybe you coulds" until finally they reached a compromise.

"Okay. Then it's a deal," Betsy said, and smiled as she got ready to leave for rehearsal. Lewis went back to bed. The thought of flying off to Never-Never Land upset his stomach, since he could barely manage to walk. The only land he wanted to visit today was dreamland.

"I'll talk to Max and Max'll talk to his father. It's up to you two boys if you want to tell his father the complete truth or not. I don't want to know. But the bottom line is that Max stays here until the show is over. Then we renegotiate. And," she added, shaking a finger at him, "you will check in with me by phone every single night and every morning. Got it?"

"G-g-got it," Lewis agreed, shaking Betsy's hand.

"And, in exchange for my cooperation, and for waking up my parents in the middle of the night, you will work your butt off in rehearsal, and you will give a brilliant performance as John Darling, garnering much critical acclaim. Right?"

"R-r-right," Lewis said. What did *garner* mean? he wondered.

"One last thing," Betsy added as she put on her helmet. "No more Superdogs."

By the time she had revved up her motorcycle and headed down the driveway, under the suspicious eye of Frances Rupert, Lewis had slipped back into a deep sleep.

14

Get to the Point, Max

MAX SHOOK HIS HEAD gravely as Lewis told him about the night before and about Betsy's deal.

"It's fascism, man, pure and simple. I say we dust her."

"D-d-dust her?"

"Yeah. Like, give her a trimming. Rearrange her face. You know."

Lewis laughed. It was Saturday, and they were sitting under a big oak tree in the woods. Max had coaxed Lewis out of the house, and now he felt a little better. His legs were still weak, though.

"Well, don't worry. I'll fix it with Phil so I can stay. I'll just tell him we have to work on our roles. He won't mind as long as I show up at home at least once a day. And maybe some nights we can stay at my house. So that solves your problem, buddy boy."

"N-not quite," Lewis said, and he told Max about the dreaded Frances Rupert catching him on Thursday, and how he'd promised to have his grandmother call her the next day.

Now it was Saturday and already a day late. That stumped even Max. He paced back and forth, then he climbed up the tree and sat on a thick branch. When he plopped back down to the ground, Lewis was beginning to lose hope. But Max had a funny look on his face. Something was up.

"W-w-what?" Lewis asked him.

"Look, you stay right here and I'll be back in about an hour. I'm gonna get the wheel on your bike fixed, and then we're gonna fix your little problem."

"How?" Lewis asked.

"Trust me. An hour," Max said, and he walked off through the woods toward the shopping center. Then he turned and grinned. "I'll bet you didn't know that Betsy is quite a talented character actress. Very accomplished with voices."

"She'll never d-d-do it," Lewis said.

"Oh, yes, she will," Max said. "She'll have to when I get through with her." He winked and then he was gone.

HANK'S SERVICE STATION was two miles down Route 22. A sign hanging from the front door read SERVING CUSTOMERS FOR OVER TWENTY YEARS. The station looked as if it hadn't been cleaned once in that time. A huge pile of tires and rusted car parts stretched clear around to the back of the station. An old tow truck was parked out front, its paint all peeled off and its cab now home to a gang of mangy stray cats and an extended family of spiders.

Hank, or "Mr. Las Vegas" as Max called him, was the owner. He wore a thick gold ring on his pinky and flowered shirts with wide collars. Hank spent most days sitting in his cluttered office with his feet up on the desk, reading magazines and talking on the phone. Today he didn't even bother to look up from his magazine when Lewis and Max rode in on their bikes, crossing the hose that made the bell ring in the office.

"The new *Playboy* must be in," Max said.

Betsy worked part time for Hank as a mechanic, and she was known as one of the best in town. People from all over brought their cars to Betsy. She had a running bet with Hank that if he could tow it to the station, she could get it to run. Betsy also pumped gas, which was supposed to be Hank's job, but once he settled into that chair and opened up a magazine, it was almost impossible to get him up again.

Lewis looked around for Betsy. An old station wagon stood in the shade of the maple trees that bordered the station. Holding a rolled-up poster, Max made his way toward it, doing his best Matt Dillon impersonation. Betsy leaned out from under the open hood. She was wearing a pair of stained gray overalls, and she had a big smudge of grease across her forehead.

"Hey, guys. What's up? You feeling better now, Lewis?" Betsy stuffed her wrench into one of the pockets in her overalls. She put her hands on the small of her back and slowly straightened up, grimacing. "I hope you guys are staying out of trouble."

"Betsy, darling, can we talk?" Max said, holding the rolled-up poster behind his back.

Betsy rubbed her hands on a rag that looked greasier than her hands. Then she reached out for Max.

"Come here and let me give you a big hug and a kiss." She smiled deviously.

"Keep those hands of death away from me and my client here," Max said, slipping out of her reach. "You are in need of some serious grease relief."

"Your client?" Betsy asked.

"Yes. Exactly. That's correct. Lewis Dee is now my client and—"

"Partner in crime is more accurate," Betsy interrupted.

"Whatever you prefer, Ms. Harris. Or may I call you 'Betsy'?" Max sounded like one of those television lawyers. But Lewis doubted that anyone could persuade Betsy to call Mrs. Rupert.

"Betsy's fine." She shot an amused glance at Lewis.

"Betsy it is, then," Max said. "As we are both aware now of my client's living situation, I wanted to stop by personally and accept your offer as it was drawn up early yesterday morning at my client's home. I have agreed to stay with him at his home until further notice and, you will be glad to know, I've already made the necessary arrangements with Phil . . . uh, rather, with my father."

"Fine," Betsy said. "You guys just better stay out of trouble or I'll—I'll make you clean up this gas station."

Max took a long, slow look around the station, winked at Lewis, and turned back to Betsy. "No, no. We certainly wouldn't want that."

"Good. Now, it's been swell, guys, but if you'll excuse me, I have to get back to work."

"Ahem . . . there is just one small, little, itsy-bitsy, teeny-weeny problem on which we will need your help," Max said.

"Problem? What problem?"

"Really, it's such a small thing, I hesitate to even use the word *problem,* but—"

"Get to the point, Max," Betsy said.

"Right. Of course. I was about to. You see, we need the very best actress these parts have to offer. So my client and I sat down and asked ourselves, 'Who can we get for this difficult role at such a late date? Who has the necessary talent and technique, not to mention beauty? Meryl Streep? Cher? Molly Ringwald?' And all of the sudden you came to mind. Betsy Harris! Of course. I couldn't help remembering that lovely—and accurate—review you received for the role of Mrs. Roosevelt two summers back. May I quote? 'A stunning performance by a young up-and-coming local talent, whom you will believe absolutely in her role as Mrs. Roosevelt. The old Mrs. Roosevelt.' "

Betsy smiled.

"Yep. That was a good review. But you added a line, Max. They didn't say 'the old Mrs. Roosevelt.' "

"Is that so? Ah, my mistake. But then, she was quite old, wasn't she?" Max said.

"Seventy-two," Betsy said.

Max turned to Lewis and mouthed the number, "Seventy-two."

"Well, look, I've got work to do," Betsy announced, as Max darted between her and the station wagon.

"Wait. You haven't heard the favor we need—"

"Max! Get to the point. I haven't got all day."

"Okay. This is it. We need you to call Lewis's next-door neighbor and pretend that you're his grandmother and say that you're staying with him and that she doesn't need to worry or call the police, who will put Lewis up for adoption or in prison or something horrible like taking him out of the play." Max took a deep breath. "That's all," he added.

"Oh, boy. I knew this arrangement wasn't going to work. I should have had my head examined for agreeing to it."

"No. It will work. You just have to make this one call, and everything will be fine. Trust me."

Max tried to sound confident, but Lewis didn't think Betsy was going to bite. He put on his best sad face, hoping that would help. What if she didn't do it? Mrs. Rupert would find out the truth. She'd make him move in with them for the rest of the summer. What could he do? He couldn't live with the Ruperts. And Bunny! Lewis stepped between Betsy and Max. "P-p-please, Betsy. I—I—I . . ."

Max put his arm around Lewis and pulled him aside. "Cool those burning jets, my friend," he said calmly, as if nothing important were at stake. He looked at Betsy again.

"No way!" she cried. "I can't lie. If she finds out, this Mrs. Whoever-she-is, she'd probably call the police. I'd be a dead duck. I'm planning on going to college next year, not to prison. It's probably like kidnapping or something."

Lewis kicked a stone and it bounced off a pile of tires. He never should have let Max convince him that this would work. What a joke. Of course Betsy wouldn't do it. She was practically an adult. Adults didn't do stuff like this.

Max cleared his throat. "Anyway, Ms. Harris—"

"Oh, so now we're back to 'Ms. Harris,' again, are we? Look, I don't care if you call me 'Your Royal Highness,' it's still no. N-O, NO!" She took her wrench out of her pocket and marched back to the station wagon.

Max tapped the rolled-up poster against his chin. "Looks like I'm going to have to use the secret weapon," he said to Lewis.

"Let's n-not and s-s-say we did," Lewis suggested. "This isn't g-going to w-w-work. I'll just tell the R-Ruperts the t-truth."

"Lost Boys never say die!" Max shouted. "Charge!" He leapt onto the rear bumper of the station wagon and, with a lot of effort, pulled himself up onto the roof. Betsy jumped back from underneath the hood.

"I didn't want to do this, Ms. Harris, but you have left me with no choice," Max announced, and he let the poster unfurl.

"Max, you get off of that—" Betsy stopped midsentence when she saw the poster. It was a huge picture of her dressed as a hippopotamus, looking absolutely foolish. She was big and fat and she had red polka dots painted all over her face. She was sticking her tongue out at the camera. It had been taken two summers ago during a production of a children's play. Max had gotten the picture blown up at the poster store in the shopping center.

"You little creep, you! Give me that!" Betsy lunged for the poster. But Max dodged her and laughed.

"There are also negatives, Ms. Harris! And I might add, they are in a safe deposit box. If anything were to happen to either myself or my client, an unnamed associate has instructions to turn the negatives over to the campus newspaper. I was also thinking that Mr. Sweet, our illustrious director, might enjoy a copy for his very own. Suitable for framing. What do you think?" Max looked down at Betsy and smiled triumphantly.

"All right, you little blackmailer, I'll do it," she said.

"I knew you'd see the light," Max said, and he handed over the poster with a courtly bow. Betsy immediately tore it to pieces.

"I'm doing this for Lewis, not because of your dumb poster," she said, reaching into her overalls for some change. "So, what's this lady's phone number? Might as well get it over with."

Max handed her a sheet of paper with Frances Rupert's name, phone number, and information about Lewis and his family that she might need for the call. Betsy looked it over, then stormed off to the phone booth.

"Somebody help me down, for crying out loud," Max yelled from the roof of the station wagon.

THE TWO BOYS waited outside the booth as Betsy took a deep breath and lifted the receiver.

"Am I your mother's mother or your father's mother?" she asked Lewis.

"Father's m-mother," he said.

Betsy turned to Max. "See, smarty, you didn't think of everything." She shut the glass door, took another deep breath, and dropped the coin in the slot.

Lewis and Max leaned close to the glass in hopes of hearing something. Lewis put a hand over his mouth to stop the nervous giggles from sneaking out. Betsy began to talk, but because of the cars passing by, the boys couldn't hear what she was saying. She did smile, and even laughed once. From what Lewis could hear, her old-lady voice was perfect. He had to keep looking up at her face to remind himself that it was Betsy. The voice didn't sound like hers at all.

Max gave him the thumbs-up sign, and they shook hands. Things were looking good. But then Betsy bit down hard on her thumbnail. She wrinkled her brow, and her voice sounded unsure. Lewis started to worry. Mrs. Rupert must have asked her one of her famous trick questions. Mrs. Rupert was a very tricky person. Maybe she was onto Betsy. And to him.

Betsy hung up the phone and slowly opened the door. She looked at both boys for a long time and shook her head before she spoke.

"I can't believe this. I just can't believe that I did it. That woman is incredible. She just talks and talks and talks."

"What happened? What'd she say?" Max asked.

"Lewis? You and your 'grandmother' are having dinner with the Ruperts. Tomorrow night," Betsy announced.

15

Grandmother Betsy

SOMEONE IN THE NEIGHBORHOOD was having a barbecue. Lewis could smell the charcoal fire and hear people shouting and splashing in a backyard swimming pool. He wished he were there instead of standing in the blue glow of the Ruperts' front-porch bug light.

He looked at Betsy, who was at his side, poised and ready to press the doorbell. If he hadn't been so nervous, Lewis would have laughed. She was dressed in a flowered dress that buttoned all the way from her neck down to her ankles. Her shoes were the kind that old people with bad feet wore. She had on long white gloves, a gray wig, glasses, and a veil to cover her face. None of her was showing! It had taken the three of them five hours in the theater costume room to put together her costume and apply her makeup.

Betsy stood hunched over, leaning on a cane. She looked at Lewis and took a deep breath.

"Are you ready?" she asked in a raspy voice.

"No," Lewis said.

"Yeah? Well, neither am I," she said. "But here goes." She closed her eyes, reached out, and pressed the doorbell. Lewis felt as if they were trick-or-treaters on Halloween night.

"Did you hear the bell?" Betsy whispered.

"No. I don't think so," Lewis said. "Maybe it's broken."

"Maybe they had to leave town suddenly." Betsy reached for the polished brass door-knocker. As she lifted it, the door flew open, pulling her halfway into the house. Mr. Rupert gave her a startled look. Betsy regained her balance with her cane, adjusted her dress, and mumbled. Bunny came bounding into the room like a rabbit and started to yap at Betsy.

"Oh, my. I'm so sorry. I really must fix that bell. Please come in," said Mr. Rupert as he tried to calm Bunny down.

Lewis followed Betsy into the Ruperts' house. The living room was cool from the air conditioner. Mr. Rupert shut the front door and turned to Betsy and Lewis with a polite smile. Lewis could tell that he was studying Betsy.

"Well . . . ah . . . can I take your . . . gloves and . . . ah, your veil?"

"Oh, no, thank you," Betsy said in a high, soft voice.

Lewis was too scared to look at Betsy directly. He knew it was his turn to talk. Betsy had instructed him on what to say if the Ruperts asked to take her veil and gloves. She needed to hide her face and hands because, even with all the makeup, they wouldn't look old close up. Betsy smiled at him, and he could see that her eyes were frantic. But before he could say anything, Mr. Rupert asked, "Are you sure I can't take your veil? It must be awfully uncomfortable in the heat and—"

Lewis touched Mr. Rupert's arm, pretending to be discreet. There was no turning back now. He thought of Max and how he never seemed to give up. The harder something was for him to do—climb a tree, run, or even jump on the roof of a station wagon—the more he seemed to want to do it. Lewis remembered Max's motto, Lost Boys never say die!

He opened his mouth. "She's ashamed of her age spots," he said without stuttering. And then, even though he would have given anything to get out of that house, he was happier than he'd been in a long time. He had just looked straight into the eyes of an adult and said an entire sentence without stuttering.

Mrs. Rupert swooped in from the kitchen. "Hello, hello, hello! Isn't this fun?" she gushed. Her jaw dropped when she saw Betsy, but she recovered with a big smile. "It's so, so nice to finally meet you, Mrs. Dee," she said. "And don't you look like a little man," she said to Lewis. She didn't take her eyes off Betsy for a second.

"How about a drink before dinner? A drop of sherry or some wine, perhaps?" Mr. Rupert suggested.

"I'd like a rum and coke," Betsy said in her best grandmother voice.

"Rum and coke?" Mrs. Rupert stared at Betsy. Lewis held his breath.

"That would be just fine," Betsy said.

"Rum and coke it is," Mr. Rupert said finally. "And how about you, sport? How about a soda?" Mr. Rupert always called Lewis "sport" and mussed up his hair as if he were a dog. Still, Mr. Rupert was better than Mrs. Rupert.

LEWIS SAT QUIETLY sipping his soda as Mrs. Rupert grilled Betsy. Betsy dodged most of the questions and held her own. She never once dropped her character or her voice. Lewis thought that she deserved an Academy Award for her performance. Mr. Rupert sat in his chair, smiling and looking back and forth. Lewis could tell that he wasn't paying attention.

He looked like one of the mechanical figures at Disney World.

Suddenly a bell went off in the kitchen, and Mrs. Rupert stood up.

"Well, that's dinner. If you'd all go into the dining room, I'll just make sure that everything is ready." She went through the swinging door into the kitchen.

Lewis and Betsy and Mr. Rupert sat down at the long dining-room table. The table was set with flowers and candles and fancy dishes. Mr. Rupert poured wine and lit the candles.

"Honey? Could you come in here and help me for a second?" Mrs. Rupert yelled from the kitchen.

As the kitchen door shut behind Mr. Rupert, Betsy guzzled the wine in front of her and refilled her glass.

"That woman is unbelievable," she whispered to Lewis. "Let's eat fast and get the hell out of here!" She took another big swig of her wine as the kitchen door swung open. Mr. and Mrs. Rupert entered carrying platters of roast beef, carrots, potatoes, and salad. It was an enormous meal for the middle of the summer, but Lewis hadn't seen so much normal food since his last meal with his parents. His mouth watered.

MRS. RUPERT TURNED TO LEWIS AND SMILED. "Well, young man, you must be enjoying this visit with your grandmother."

"Yes. Yes, I am," Lewis said a little too heartily.

"More meat, sport?" Mr. Rupert asked.

"No, thank you," he answered. He looked at Betsy, who seemed to be leaning to one side of her chair. She was smiling and trying to eat a carrot through her veil. Lewis realized she was drunk.

"More roast beef for you, Mrs. Dee?" Mr. Rupert asked.

Betsy didn't even answer him. She just kept smiling and trying to get her food around her veil.

"By the way," Mrs. Rupert said suddenly, "I saw a motorbike in your driveway the other morning. To whom does it belong?"

"To me," said Betsy, without thinking.

Lewis pretended to drop his napkin and dived under the table. When he peeked up, Mr. and Mrs. Rupert were both staring at Betsy.

"That is, I do own it, but, of course, I'd never ride such a noisy, dangerous vehicle," Betsy told them. "In all honesty, I bought the motorcycle for my . . . ah . . . my . . . daughter."

Mrs. Rupert frowned. She set her knife and fork down. "You bought a motorbike for your daughter?" She smiled suspiciously. "I didn't know that you had a daughter. Lewis's father never mentioned a sister. Where is she now?"

"Well, she wanted it so badly, and I can never seem to deny my children a thing. Besides, I don't see any reason for a young woman not to ride a motorcycle, do you?" Betsy deftly sidestepped Mrs. Rupert's questions by asking one of her own, Lewis realized. He'd have to learn to do that.

"I suppose not," Mrs. Rupert reluctantly agreed.

"I don't know. Women and motorcycles? Who wants more meat?" Mr. Rupert asked.

DESSERT WAS STRAWBERRY SHORTCAKE, with lots of whipped cream. Lewis ate every bite on his plate. Just as Mrs. Rupert was about to offer him more, Betsy spoke up. By now she was slurring her words, but it was hard to notice with her disguised voice. And the veil.

"I am sorry to have to eat and run. It's terribly impolite, I know. But I do get tired so early on these hot summer nights."

"Of course, dear." Mrs. Rupert smiled. "I'm just so glad you were able to join us. Us girls will have to get together some afternoon soon for a nice luncheon."

"Yes, that would be nice, wouldn't it," Betsy said.

Mr. Rupert walked them to the end of the driveway and watched as they crossed the street.

"Hold me up," Betsy whispered as they made their way up the stairs to the front porch and opened the front door. Max was waiting for them.

"What happened? Disaster city, or what?" he asked anxiously as Betsy collapsed onto the sofa with a loud groan. "I knew it wouldn't work. What a terrible idea!"

"It did w-work," Lewis told him.

"Hey, hey, I knew it. I knew it. I never had a moment's doubt. I had complete faith in you guys," Max said. He looked at Betsy. "Bet you need a good strong drink right now, huh?"

"Two aspirin is more like it. Could you get them for me, please?"

Lewis got the aspirin, and Betsy, still in her disguise, fell asleep on the sofa. But Lewis and Max stayed up until almost midnight, as Lewis acted out a moment-by-moment replay of the evening. And then, finally, they fell asleep too.

16

Disaster City

"I'M NOT EATING any of these fiddlesticks. I don't care how much they cost." Max pushed his plate away and glared at his father.

Lewis stared at the strange-looking green things curled up on his dish. They looked like things he stepped on in the woods.

"Fiddleheads, not fiddlesticks, you ungrateful culinary creep of a kid. They're ferns and they're very hard to get ahold of, so you'd better eat them or I'm cutting you out of my will." Phil patted his son on the head. "And if I catch you slipping even one of those scrumptious little buds to Rex the Wonder Dog, I'm putting you on the first bus back to New York City. I hear it's real pleasant there in August."

Max grumbled, stabbed a fiddlehead with his fork, and popped it into his mouth. Lewis did the same. It didn't taste so bad. Despite the weird food, Lewis enjoyed eating dinner with Phil. He was a lot more fun than the Ruperts.

"Maybe you'll learn some manners from Lewis this

summer," Phil suggested to his son, as he carried a bowl of unidentifiable food to the table. "I hope you're behaving better in front of his parents. It's a wonder they're allowing you to stay there every night."

Max and Lewis exchanged a look. They dutifully cleaned their plates, then left for the evening rehearsal.

Opening night was only a week away, so now they were rehearsing all day and evenings too. Everybody was working hard. The sets were almost all up. The dances and musical numbers were coming together. Costumes were being fitted, and people were actually remembering their lines.

Lewis was completely caught up in the excitement. Betsy had worked hard with him on his dialogue, bringing his stutter under control. It didn't seem nearly as bad when he was saying words that he had memorized as when he talked normally, trying to get out what he was thinking. Now he felt confident and he had all but forgotten his troubles. Until his troubles remembered him.

The rehearsal, a full run-through without costumes or lights, was taking a long time because they kept having to stop for one problem or another. The big flying number was at the end of the first act, when Peter Pan comes to take Wendy, John, and Michael Darling back to Never-Never Land. Lewis and Betsy had to grab hands at one point while they were twenty feet off the ground, then join hands with Eddie, the little boy playing Michael Darling. Then they had to fly out the nursery window together, singing all the while.

Lewis was getting tired, but Mr. Sweet kept running the number over and over, trying to get it right. The last time, Betsy had flown right into the set wall and knocked it over. While they stopped to fix the set, Lewis turned and saw what appeared to be a face in the window at the far, dark end of the auditorium. It disappeared so fast that he thought he was imagining it. He looked again. No face.

Minutes later, as Lewis grabbed Betsy's hand in midair and they flew out the nursery window with Eddie, he glanced around and there it was again. The face. A boy's face. No. Wait. . . . It was familiar. It was Stanley Flynn! He was sure of it. But then Lewis flew out the window, and he was behind the set wall. By the time he was unhooked from his harness and ran around to the front of the stage, the face was gone.

Later, when they were all leaving rehearsal, Lewis almost went over to see if there were footprints in the dirt or if the plants had been trampled below the window. But he didn't want to know for sure. After all, he could have imagined it.

"TUNA SPAGHETTI?" Lewis was doubtful.

"Hey, trust me," Max said as he danced around Lewis's kitchen, stirring and grating and measuring and chopping up the ingredients for dinner. "Aren't I the son of a locally famous chef?"

Lewis wasn't sure that Max had inherited Phil's culinary skills, but he was so hungry that he didn't really care. He went into the dining room to dismantle the tent. With his parents coming home in two weeks he and Max had been spending part of each night cleaning up the house. It was a big job, but so far it was looking good. Betsy had even pitched in last Sunday, helping them wax the kitchen floor and giving them advice on the harder jobs. In spite of all the messes they had made, nothing was broken or damaged, except for the drainpipe.

"Here, cool your tubes with a couple of sippers of this specialty of the house." Max produced a bottle of California Cooler from his day pack.

"Where'd you g-get that?" Lewis asked him.

"Just a small bottle, to celebrate, my friend. A toast to our successes. Broadway, here we come!" Max jumped up on top of the kitchen table and held the bottle to his chest. "Ladies and gentlemen, members of the Academy, I'd like to thank you for this award. Words seem curiously inappropriate right now, but I must say that I couldn't have done it without my brilliant director, and without my father, my mother, my dog Rex, and all of the little people behind the scenes on whom I stepped on my way to the top."

Lewis applauded.

"And of course," Max continued, "that great rising star of the American, nay, the international, theater and film scene, who was a great inspiration to me . . . Lewis Dee!"

"Bravo! Bravo!" Lewis threw vegetables at Max, who naturally threw them back, and soon there was a full-fledged food fight in progress.

Finally they sat down to a dinner of overcooked, mushy spaghetti and canned tomato sauce with tuna fish mixed in and topped with grated cheddar cheese.

"It t-tastes sort of like b-bad pizza," Lewis said.

Dessert was a real peach pie, baked by Frances Rupert. She had been regularly leaving food, mostly cakes and pies, with notes to Lewis's grandmother, on the front porch.

And the California Cooler, of course. Max, being thirteen and a New Yorker, was a seasoned drinker. He had been "blasted," so he said, many times. But Lewis had never had more than a can of beer. He ended up sacked out on the living room floor while Max washed the dinner dishes, singing all the Broadway songs he knew.

"HOIST ME HIGHER. Get me up higher, you idiots!" Stanley Flynn hissed in the dark as Cycle and Wanker pulled on the thick rope that lifted Flynn, strapped into the harness, high above the stage.

"Hold your stupid horses or we'll drop you on your ugly

face," Cycle warned him, jerking the rope to remind Flynn who was in charge at the moment.

"Keep it down, you guys," whispered another voice out of the darkness. Cheese.

It was difficult to see anything in the theater. The only light came from the glowing exit signs and the flashlights they carried. But the sounds of their mischief left nothing to the imagination. They laughed as knives ripped through canvas backdrops, fists punched holes in scenery walls, and spray paint hissed, covering everything.

Suddenly the theater lights went on.

"What's going on here?" an angry voice shouted. A campus security guard stood in the doorway.

"Run for it!" Cheese yelled.

Campus police poured in the door while Flynn's gang ran in every direction, causing even more damage as they scattered.

Cycle and Wanker ran with the others. Unfortunately for Flynn the last thing they thought about was the rope in their hands.

In the middle of all this bedlam came a blood-curdling scream. Everyone, hoodlum and policeman alike, stopped and looked up as Stanley Flynn plummeted down from the ceiling. He hit the stage floor with a thud.

Of course, none of his "friends" stopped to help him. In less than a minute the vandalized theater was completely empty, except for the campus police and Flynn. He was sprawled out on the stage like a broken puppet, moaning with pain.

IT TOOK THE AMBULANCE MEDICS and the security police almost half an hour to get Flynn onto a stretcher and into the ambulance. He wasn't that badly hurt, just a broken collarbone, but he wouldn't stop yelling.

When the ambulance finally pulled away and all was quiet again, a security guard went back in to turn out the lights in the theater. Looking around at the destruction, he shook his head sadly, then went to the telephone to call Norman Sweet. It didn't look as if *Peter Pan* would open at the end of the week, if ever.

17

Max Understands

THE NEXT MORNING, Max and a slightly hung over Lewis bicycled to the theater. The cast and crew were gathered on the front stairs, and nobody looked very happy. Lewis thought that everyone stared at him as they rode up. Maybe he was just paranoid. Or maybe it was a byproduct of his hangover, like his headache and the awful taste in his mouth.

"What's the good word?" Max asked. Mr. Sweet pointed to the theater door and motioned Lewis and Max inside.

LEWIS BLINKED as if the horrible vision that greeted him was a mistake. But it didn't go away. His hangover took a backseat to his horror. Each detail stood out clearly. The slashed scenery and the shattered props etched a permanent picture in his brain. Worst of all, Lewis's name was spray-painted all over the walls and the floor, as if he were the vandal who had boastfully left his mark.

Lewis knew that Max was staring at him, but he couldn't

bear to look at his friend. Then he felt a hand on his shoulder. It was Betsy.

"We know who did it, Lewis, and no one blames you." She hugged him. *No one blames you* was one of those statements that really meant the opposite, Lewis knew. All the kids outside probably blamed him plenty.

"It was a boy from your school. The same boy who was here with his friends that day. Stanley Flynn."

Flynn. Of course. Flynn would follow him to the ends of the earth, it seemed. So that he wouldn't start to cry, Lewis silently repeated to himself, *Lost Boys never say die. Lost Boys never say die. Lost Boys never say die.* He said it over and over again in his mind, even though it looked as if Flynn had really won this time. The theater was ruined. Flynn had managed to wreck the one time in Lewis's life when he had felt happy and accepted.

As the rest of the kids filed quietly inside, Max growled, "We'll fry his ass for this one."

"Max!" Betsy shook her head.

"Well, at least let us put hot bamboo shoots under his fingernails."

"Max, enough!" Betsy said.

Lewis was barely listening. Their voices seemed to be coming from somewhere far away.

"Frying him won't be necessary," Mr. Sweet said, coming up behind Lewis and Max. "He's being amply punished for his crime already."

"Ha! How?" Max asked.

"It seems that he and his friends were fooling around with the harness and ropes last night. He fell and broke his collarbone. He's in the hospital right now."

"It's a start," Max conceded.

"The college is pressing charges," Betsy added. "This Flynn kid, it seems, has been in trouble with the police before. He's headed straight for juvenile court. And the police said they'll pick up the rest of the gang easy. So that takes care of them."

"Why don't we go take a walk outside, Lewis," Mr. Sweet said, and he put a hand on Lewis's shoulder. Lewis still hadn't said one word. He didn't know if he would be able to.

"I'm coming too," Max said.

"No. Why don't you stay here with me and help organize the cleanup?" Betsy suggested. Her tone left no room for argument.

Mr. Sweet led Lewis out the front doors of the theater. They walked slowly along the brick sidewalk, through the old college. Mr. Sweet seemed to be waiting for him to speak, but Lewis felt worse than ever. Even if he could talk, what could he say? *I'm sorry?* But he hadn't done anything wrong.

"I know this is going to sound odd, Lewis, but you should feel sorry for Stanley Flynn," Mr. Sweet said. "He must be a very, very unhappy boy to do the things he does."

"B-b-b-but, h-he r-r-r . . ." Lewis gave up. His stutter hadn't been this bad since school.

"We'll get the show on. Don't you worry about that. We may have to do without some of the set, but we'll get it up there. The question is, are you still with us? Are you going to be our John Darling?"

Lewis didn't answer. If he stayed, what would stop Flynn's gang from coming back and doing worse things? Sure, Flynn was in the hospital, and the rest of the gang was in trouble, but maybe it was time to give up. He couldn't burden his friends with this—this curse. A curse like the ones in the comic books he'd read. Anywhere he went, he would bring destruction and disaster down on people. He probably shouldn't even be friends with Max, for that matter. He should just go and live in a cave in the mountains by himself so that no more harm would come to anyone else.

"Look, why don't you take the afternoon off?" Mr. Sweet said. "There won't be any rehearsal, anyway. I know how you must feel."

I know how you must feel. Why did grown-ups always say that? How could he possibly know how Lewis felt? It made him mad when grown-ups said that.

"Whatever you decide is all right by us," Mr. Sweet said. "But we would like you with us. You're an important part of this show, Lewis. I want you to know that." Mr. Sweet patted him on the back. "Well, I'd better get back inside. We'll see you tomorrow?"

Lewis shrugged, but he didn't say anything as Mr. Sweet walked back to the theater.

"Psst."

Lewis looked around.

"Is he gone?" The voice was coming from behind a garbage bin, next to the cafeteria building.

"W-w-what?" Lewis said.

Max popped out from behind the bin. His sleeves were rolled all the way up to his shoulders and he was wearing a football helmet. He was carrying two long sticks, a can of paint, and a big bag filled with who-knows-what. Lewis was afraid to guess.

"Revenge City!" Max yelled. "We are going to do a major Charles Bronson on those creeps. I got it all figured out."

Max described the torture he had planned, which he'd seen in some old movie about Rome. The Romans had taken their enemies and buried them alive with just their heads sticking out of the ground. Then they covered them with honey, so that bugs and birds would come and eat them alive.

"Slowly," Max said, grinning. "Then, when they were

almost dead, they'd run over their heads with their horses to finish them off. Neat, huh?"

Lewis didn't say anything, although it did sound like a great idea. He walked over to the bike rack and unlocked his bike.

"Hey, what's wrong? Mr. Sweet-and-sour didn't kick you out of the show, did he?"

"N-n-no."

"What, then? You don't like the torture? I got another idea. It involves a train and some rope. It's great. Or there's one I saw in a pirate movie, but we'd need a ship and an ocean. That would take too much time. I say we go with the Roman one."

Lewis wished he could really tell Max how he felt. But he was afraid that he couldn't even get the words out without taking an hour.

"M-M-Max?"

"Yeah, buddy?"

"You d-d-d-don't underst-st-st-stand w-what . . ."

"I don't understand? I don't understand! Is that what you're going to say? That I don't understand what it's like for you?"

Lewis nodded.

"I don't understand. Hah! You listen up, man, and listen good. I've spent my entire life being called every name that was ever thought up for 'fat.' And then some. Dumbo. Tubby. Fatso. Blimpo. There isn't one I haven't heard. So don't go telling me that I don't understand." Max stopped to catch his breath. "But you can't let them get to you, or else they've won." He put his arm around Lewis. "Listen, I'll tell you something in confidence if you promise not to repeat it."

Lewis nodded. "Sh-sure."

"I don't really think I'm the next Tom Cruise. But if I don't say it, who will?"

"I—I—I—" Lewis started to speak, but he was interrupted by an angry voice from the top of the theater steps.

"Max Winkler! You get those props, and yourself, back into the theater on the double. Pronto!" Mr. Sweet yelled.

"Uh-oh. It's Sweet-and-sour himself. I'd better shake a leg," Max said. "Look, Lewis, I can't tell you what to do, but I think you ought to follow me up those stairs. We need you. And you need us too."

Max turned and walked back up into the theater.

Lewis knew Max was right. He'd never change his stutter, or his life, if he didn't try to do something about it himself. It was his life, and nobody—not Max, not Betsy—was going to live it for him.

Lewis looked up at the theater doors, took a deep breath, and marched up the stairs.

18

Really Flying

THE NIGHT BEFORE OPENING NIGHT, Lewis and Max were both too nervous to sleep. They sat at the kitchen table for hours, going over Lewis's lines again and again, until even Lewis got sick of it. Then, because Lewis's parents were due home the next week, they finished cleaning up the house.

"I think it looks pretty good," Max said, as they made a final inspection through the house, room by room. All the furniture and pillows and cushions and books were back in place. The tent was gone from the dining room, and the little house under the table had been dismantled. "It looks just like a normal, boring house to me."

"It's n-not boring," Lewis said.

"Aw, you know what I mean. It looks like parents live here."

Lewis nodded. "Yeah. I d-don't think th-they'll be able to t-t-tell."

"But what are you gonna tell them when they get back and they find out you didn't go to camp?" Max opened up the refrigerator, ready to make their fourth snack of the night.

"I—I don't know," Lewis said, as he helped Max carry jars and bottles to the kitchen table. Max liked to spread out absolutely every kind of food that was available, and then have a little taste of each one.

"Well, they'll probably be so happy to see you, and so excited about the play, that they won't be too, too mad," Max said.

"Maybe," Lewis agreed. But he wasn't worried about his parents. He was too excited and nervous about the play to think of anything else. For the first time he understood what "butterflies in your stomach" meant. He felt like he had an entire flock flying around in there. Possibly a few caterpillars too.

IT WAS OPENING NIGHT, and Lewis felt like a completely different person. Maybe it was the lack of sleep. All day long he had been walking around the house in a fog. But when he arrived at the theater, he didn't feel tired at all. Instead, everything seemed, well . . . more intense. Bigger, brighter, and louder. It was as if he were living inside of a television picture, and someone had adjusted the color and the sound. The grass on the lawn in front of the theater had never looked so bright a green. And when he and Max walked inside and he heard the orchestra warming up, Lewis could hear every instrument.

"Hey, I gotta go call Phil. Tell him where I left his ticket for tonight," Max said, heading down the center aisle. "I'll catch you later, okay?"

"Okay," Lewis said. The crew was setting up rows of chairs, and suddenly Lewis realized that hundreds and hundreds of people were going to be there that night, watching him onstage. He had known it all along, but actually seeing the chairs made it real. Lewis wasn't scared anymore. He was excited. This was a challenge and he was ready.

"Max?" he shouted. But Max was already gone. Lewis went downstairs to the dressing room he shared with Eddie, who played his little brother, Michael Darling. Max was in a bigger dressing room with all the Lost Boys.

Two big gold stars were taped to the door, and they had Lewis's and Eddie's names written on them. Lewis went in, and Eddie was already there, sitting in front of the mirror. One of the older girls in charge of costumes was helping him put on his stage makeup. Eddie gave Lewis the thumbs-up sign. Lewis returned it and sat down on the other side of the room at his own table. A big envelope was propped up against the mirror. He opened it and pulled out a card, with a hand-drawn picture of a boy flying over the theater on the front. *To my favorite flyer. You're going to be great. See you in Never-Never Land. Love, Betsy.*

"OKAY. PLACES, EVERYBODY." Mr. Sweet, dressed in a suit and clutching his clipboard, was running around in circles backstage, frantically trying to get everybody ready. On the other side of the curtain Lewis could hear the audience quieting down. Then there was loud applause as the college orchestra began to play the overture.

"That's it," said the stagehand who was helping Lewis into his leather harness. He gave one last tug on the strap and Lewis felt it tighten around his waist. No one would see the harness because it was underneath Lewis's costume, which was an old-fashioned nightshirt.

Eddie, wearing funny little-boy's pajamas with the feet attached, was standing next to Lewis, having his harness adjusted too. Eddie was holding a teddy bear. Lewis wished he had something to hold. He was getting scared again. His heart was pounding and he was breathing fast, and his legs were tingling and weak. Lewis had never felt so strange. One minute he was excited, and the next minute he was scared. Then excited again. Then scared. He wished his body would make up its mind.

"Here we go," a voice said, and Betsy was there, holding both of their hands. She looked beautiful in her costume, a long pink nightgown. "Let's give these folks their money's worth."

Before Lewis even had time to think, he heard the overture come to an end. The curtain started to rise. And the audience applauded again. The next thing he knew, he was out onstage.

It was a different world, nothing like it had been in rehearsal! The lights were so bright that he couldn't see the audience. It was as if he were moving around in a glass bowl. And inside the bowl it didn't look like a stage in a theater anymore. It was a real nursery in a real house. Outside the big nursery window was London, England. The stars in the sky were twinkling. When the guy who played Mr. Darling, their father, came in, Lewis opened his mouth to speak. And it wasn't Lewis talking, but his character, John Darling. All the lines came out perfectly. Betsy turned to him and smiled, and she was his big sister, Wendy Darling.

Lewis felt like he was in a dream, but he knew he wasn't dreaming. He could watch and listen but still be outside it. And, as in a dream, time seemed to move twice as fast. Soon Lewis was lying in his nursery bed, pretending to be asleep, and he heard the big nursery window blow open with a *whoosh* of air. Everyone in the audience gasped, and he knew that Peter Pan had flown in the window.

* * *

"PETER, CAN YOU REALLY FLY?" Lewis asked Peter Pan. Wendy, John, and Michael were all awake now. They were listening to Peter tell them stories of Never-Never Land, of pirates and Indians, and of all the adventures he and the Lost Boys had every day.

"I'll teach you," Peter Pan said. The next thing Lewis knew, he and Betsy and Eddie were jumping off their beds and soaring around the nursery, singing "I'm Flying." Lewis landed on top of the fireplace mantel, and Betsy flew over to join him. The nursery windows blew open again, and Peter Pan was leading them away. Betsy and Lewis sailed into the air, joined hands with Eddie, and together they flew out in the starry London night.

Lewis forgot that he was attached to a wire. He felt as if he were really flying, high above the earth. Betsy squeezed his hand tight. Lewis looked down and saw Max, hidden in the wings, waving up at them, and he started to laugh. As the curtain came down and everyone started to clap, Lewis laughed and laughed for a long time.

Note to the Reader

Stuttering can be a seemingly overwhelming obstacle in life or a challenge to be overcome. Approximately one percent of all school-age children stutter. While nobody knows exactly what causes it or how to cure it, we do know that stuttering occurs more often in boys than girls; that seventy-five percent of all children will outgrow it without professional treatment; and that stuttering is not a psychological disorder. Although anxiety does make stuttering worse, people who stutter are, on the whole, no more anxious than anyone else. A speech-language pathologist should be consulted when stuttering persists for six to twelve months.

In *Lost Boys Never Say Die* Lewis, an eleven-year-old boy who stutters, discovers that he can sing fluently even before an audience and that acting affords him another fluent experience. He also learns that self-assertion can conquer fear. Reduced fear often leads to enhanced fluency. Such risk-taking and self-realizations are important steps toward remediation. This story may serve as an inspiration for children who must learn to cope with the physical and emotional challenges of a speech impairment.

Dianne Slavin, M.A., CCC/Sp
Director, Speech and Hearing Dept.
ICD—International Center
for the Disabled, New York, New York

About the Authors

ALAN BROWN is the recipient of a 1987–88 Fulbright Fellowship in Journalism and a 1988 New York Foundation for the Arts Fiction Award. His fiction has appeared in *Seventeen* magazine and other well-known publications. He has written for network television, and his plays have been staged in New York City and aired on National Public Radio. He is a regular contributor to major newspapers and magazines, including the *Los Angeles Times. Lost Boys Never Say Die* is his first novel.

Mr. Brown lives in Tokyo and in New York City.

GRANT FORSBERG is the director of development for an independent film company that is part of Columbia Pictures Entertainment, Inc. He started his acting and writing career at the Neighborhood Playhouse School of Dramatic Arts in New York City, and has appeared in soap operas, nighttime television, and movies. *Lost Boys Never Say Die* is his first novel.

Mr. Forsberg lives in Los Angeles, California.